NORTH TO MONTANA

Steven C. Lawrence

D0001356

Chivers Press
Bath, England
Thorndike Press
Waterville, Maine USA

This Large Print edition is published by Chivers Press, England, and by Thorndike Press, USA.

Published in 2002 in the U.K. by arrangement with the author c/o Golden West Literary Agency.

Published in 2002 in the U.S. by arrangement with Golden West Literary Agency.

U.K. Hardcover ISBN 0–7540–7444–7 (Chivers Large Print)
U.K. Softcover   ISBN 0–7540–7445–5 (Camden Large Print)
U.S. Softcover   ISBN 0–7862–4486–0 (Nightingale Series Edition)

The text of this Large Print edition is unabridged.
Other aspects of the book may vary from the original edition.

Set in 16 pt. New Times Roman.

Printed in Great Britain on acid-free paper.

British Library Cataloguing in Publication Data available

Library of Congress Cataloging-in-Publication Data

Lawrence, Steven C.
    North to Montana / Steven C. Lawrence.
       p.   cm.
    ISBN 0–7862–4486–0 (lg. print : sc : alk. paper)
    1. Cattle drives—Fiction. 2. Large type books. I. Title.
PS3562.A916 N6 2002
813'.54—dc21   2002071998

CHAPTER ONE

Tom Slattery stopped his black gelding on the rise of land where the mountain trail led out through a brief foothill passage. He had known the Calligan Valley was here. Every one of the twelve-hundred hard, hot, dusty miles of the trail drive from Central Texas, he had been sure of that. Fred McDonald and Ian Huffaker had described it often enough to Slattery and the other cattlemen and their wives and families: long, unbroken miles and miles of virgin rangeland, brownish-green with grass stretching away to the north and west, its entire length watered by the lazy sweep of the Calligan River flowing down from the distant sheltering windbreaks of the Madison and Gallatin Mountains.

It was still more than Slattery had thought it would be. The southern pass was behind them. They had ridden for hours between low walls of dark timber, sweating in the close heat, covered with the dust kicked up by the slow-moving herd, and they were always aware of the smell of burning grass carried on the ever-present wind of Montana Territory. Slattery broke from the shade of the squaw pines and lodge poles. Smoke was visible far off toward the Gallatins, foglike and wispy over the solid stretch of bottomlands, the haze drifting on

1

the breeze and vanishing along mid-valley to leave only its telltale odor against the blinding immensity of raw blue sky and diamond-bright late September sunshine.

Slattery eased forward in the saddle, taking the strain of his weight from the tired muscles of his back. Three miles ahead the buildings which he knew made up the Gibson homestead sat gray and baking in the heat. Slattery had expected McDonald or Huffaker would have appeared from one of the ranch buildings by now. The two men had left the herd ten days ago to ride ahead and contact Gibson and the other ranchers of the valley. But there was nothing Slattery could see except the outhouse behind the small shack Gibson used as a home, a half-finished barn, and two horses in a pole corral.

The lead steers had passed Slattery, the point riders letting the tired, thirsty beeves make their own time. One of the younger punchers gave out a wild Rebel yell at seeing the endless stretch of thick growth of priceless grass. Augustin Vierra, hazing an old mossy-back Longhorn into the strung-out line, waved one arm high in the air and called to Slattery.

'It is all Fred and Ian have said. This will be our home, Thomãs.' He grinned widely, his teeth white against his dark olive skin. 'You want them stopped at the ranch?'

'No. A mile this side,' Slattery called back. 'Gibson will need his own grass, the way it's

2

been. Leave him plenty graze.'

The Mexican waved and rode ahead.

Slattery stared across the herd, watching Mat Weaver and Frank Shields, barely visible in the dust, push the steers forward. They had the boy, Jackie Pruitt, with them. Before the drive started, his father and brother had been killed and he had been left for dead. Lottie Wells and Judy Fiske had nursed him back to health, then Weaver, Shields, and Ian Huffaker took the fourteen-year-old orphan in with their families. Of the eighteen families which had headed north from Texas, eleven were still together. Three families had dropped out at Dodge City, where more than a thousand beeves of the herd had been sold. The other four families had broken off at the Platte, choosing to settle in Nebraska instead of Montana. The last of the thirty-four-hundred head they had brought here would take another two hours to move down into the valley.

Slattery's stare shifted to the drag a mile behind him. The wagons had been held back, well clear of the thick dust. Slattery's pocket watch read nine-thirty. It would be close to noon before they were in and set up for chuck. Steve Murfee, riding toward him now, realized that as well. And he would be just as concerned for McDonald and Huffaker . . .

Slattery drew the makings from the pocket of his sweat-stained gray shirt. He rolled the

3

cigarette on his lips, liking the taste of the tobacco but not fully enjoying it. He was a big man, deep-chested, and had the hard-boned, tight face of a desert rider. He had trail-bossed the drive every mile from the Red. He hadn't lost a man or woman or child of the families which had trusted him to lead in their move from the drought-stricken Texas flats. He'd made them a good profit in Union greenbacks through the Dodge City sell. They had money to buy land and supplies, plenty of cattle to market or barter, and they had kept their own stockers. Still, he didn't feel sure. Not with McDonald and Huffaker two days overdue.

The cigarette tasted stale and dry. Slattery crushed it out against the saddle horn. He shoved his gray flat-crowned hat up on his forehead, and rubbed one hand over his weather-burned, stubbled jaw.

Steve Murfee reined in his big buckskin alongside the black gelding. Murfee was in his late twenties, ten years younger than Slattery. He was as tall and leathery, and had the same easy, slow motion of a capable stockman. He looked beyond the point at the small ranch, then further on past the tree-lined river that blocked any view of Yellowstone City.

'Not one sign of Fred and Ian?' he asked flatly.

Slattery shook his head. 'Nothing. I figured at least one of them would ride out to meet us once we started in here.' He stared southward.

4

The cattle, strung out and moving too slow, threw up too much dust. Canby would keep the remuda a good distance behind the drag. The wagons would lag further behind and wouldn't be in until after noontime. Things would take longer than he'd planned. 'How about Huffaker's wife?'

'She keeps askin',' said Murfee. He watched Slattery. He knew the man's softness, but also the competent toughness that was ingrained and deep, yet without cruelty. He nodded toward the man who had stepped out of the ranchhouse at the edge of the broad valley. 'Fred was good enough friends with Gibson to wait with him.'

Slattery had also seen the man. His figure was small in the distance, too small to be either McDonald or Huffaker.

'I'll go down alone,' Slattery said. 'You keep them movin', Steve. Tell Mrs. Huffaker.'

'I will. Judy and Lottie are stayin' close, to help.' He stared beyond the flowing expanse of grass to the mountains. A line of dark clouds showed along the snowy peaks, making them loom up higher and straighter than they actually were. They were not rain clouds, he knew, but smoke, wind-blown up from a timber or grass fire somewhere in the Gallatin Valley beyond the divide. He began to turn his horse. 'I'll bring them in, Tom.'

Slattery nodded, knowing he could depend on Murfee. He kneed his gelding ahead, more concerned now that he thought of Huffaker's wife and daughters. Worry tightened the muscles of his stomach, gnawing at him. He was afraid of what he might find. He was afraid for Susan Huffaker and her two little girls.

The valley had fooled him, in a way. The grass was here all right, most of it strong and lush close to the river. But the green turned more and more brownish as it receded from the streambed. Slattery and everyone else in the drive knew firsthand the heat and pressures of the almost completely rainless summer. They'd had just two storms since fording the Arkansas, and one had been a thunder and lightning cloudburst which was over in a quarter-hour. Almost every day during the past week they'd seen a grass fire or smelled its smoke. Here, the Calligan's water sustained the land, but the closer Slattery rode to Gibson's spread, the more he noted the way the channel had receded, leaving caked mudflats along both banks. He fully understood the fires. His concern deepened about that. Every inch of graze that was burned out would deprive cattle of winter range. From what he had heard, they'd need this entire valley to supply grass once the storms began and the polar winds blew down from the wide-open stretches of Canada.

Ernest Gibson was a scrawny little man of fifty-three. An entire life of ranching had

6

sloughed off all his excess flesh years ago, leaving a leather-tough shell with thin gray hair, a bony nose, thin lips, and work-bent shoulders. He did not move from the front of his house while Slattery rode in. To Slattery the small homesteader seemed as tired and weather-worn as the dried-out pine logs of the ranch buildings.

The little man smiled when Slattery dismounted and introduced himself. For such a thin frame, Gibson had a firm, powerful handshake. He nodded toward the dust cloud made by the longhorn herd.

'You kinda surprised us,' he said, glancing across his shoulder at the house. 'Fred McDonald told me a year 'go he'd let us know 'head of time so's we could be ready for you people.'

'Fred didn't stop here?' Slattery asked.

'No.' The rancher took a step toward the house. His wife, a coarse-featured and heavy woman, watched from the doorway of the building. Three children, two boys and a girl, none older than six, hung bashfully around her apron and skirt. All studied Slattery hopefully. Even the children's faces were drawn and serious.

Slattery said, 'Fred McDonald and another of our men left the herd ten days ago.' Gibson halted. He faced Slattery as the tall Texan added, 'You were the first man they were going to see, Mr. Gibson. Have you been away from here at all?'

Gibson's bony head began to shake. His wife spoke from the doorway. 'We've waited here every day for you. Fred McDonald or nobody else hasn't come. They haven't been in Yellowstone, or Myron Blumberg would have sent word.' She jerked her head at her husband. 'What about the cows, Ern? Ask about the cows.'

Ernest Gibson snapped, 'I'll handle this, Milly. I will.' His steady stare met Slattery's. 'I been friends with Fred since we was younguns in Missouri. He wouldn't've stopped off at another town. He was bringin' your herd right here. We depended upon it. We need it.'

'This valley is where we mean to settle,' said Slattery. He glanced from the herd's dust to the smoke, darker above the mountains. He nodded to the rancher, included the family. 'I'll be back.'

'We'll get the cows, won't we?' Gibson asked.

'Yes. We'll have the herd in by tonight. But wait until tomorrow. We won't be moving until then.'

Gibson nodded. He hesitated while Slattery climbed into the saddle. His wife coughed, and the little rancher added quickly, 'Mr. Slattery, I'd agreed with Fred to take fifty or a hundred head. I can't now.' He raised one arm and motioned at the land between himself and the river. 'I had twenty head but they got into loco weed. I didn't have anything to back up a loan and the bank'd only lend me enough to pay for twenty head. All right if I just take twenty?'

Nodding, Slattery said, 'There are other spreads, Mr. Gibson. We'll see what we can do. If we have any selling stock left over, I'll see if you can take some on trust.' He started to swing his mount.

Gibson walked along beside the gelding. 'That's what I been tryin' to say.' He motioned toward the haze of smoke. 'We've never had a summer like this. Or early fall. Never so dry. So many sun fires. Other owners've lost their herds or their springs dried up to nothin' but dust and alkali. Ralph Goodlove's tried to help, but there just ain't the money. You people plan to sell your cows, you'll have to do most everythin' on tick.'

'Well, we'll see,' Slattery told him. He swung the gelding and rode at a lope southward. The sale of the excess of the herd was important. His families had depended on the money they would earn to buy land and wood to build their homes and outbuildings.

But at the moment that problem was secondary. McDonald had said he and Ian Huffaker would wait at the Gibsons' if they weren't back to the herd within a week. It was ten days, almost eleven, and neither man had even reached here.

Slattery wasn't sure how he'd tell Susan Huffaker.

CHAPTER TWO

Susan Huffaker had feared that something had happened to her husband. She'd had the feeling every minute of the two days Ian was overdue. She had no proof, except that he hadn't returned when he'd said he would. Both Ian and Fred McDonald could have been detained talking business with Ernie Gibson or the land agent in Yellowstone City. After all, she'd been married to Ian more than ten years, and a woman comes to know a man after that long. She knew how Ian liked to talk. How many times had she waited in a neighbor's house down home in Texas, late at night, with everyone wanting to go to bed but not able to because Ian and one of the other men kept talking? How many meals had grown cold or burned because he'd met a neighbor along the San Saba Road on his way home from a day in town? She'd had to tell him so many times, to get after him, even to shout at him. But this time she was too worried. This time she knew she wouldn't shout at him if she saw him coming through the valley entrance. She took hold of herself. She couldn't show her fear to her daughters on the wagon seat beside her. She simply smiled at Tom Slattery when he rode in alongside the carreta and shook her head.

'He'll meet us,' she told Slattery quietly. She was a tall, heavy-set woman, her shoulders held square and straight while she stopped the mules. Ahead of them the remuda kicked up dust that made her six-year-old Janie cough. Gayle, eighteen months older than her sister, watched Judy Fiske's big Conestoga freight wagon leave the line to pull in close to them.

'Mommy, has something happened to Daddy?' Janie asked. She pressed her small head against her mother's arm.

'No. No, of course not, dear. You know how your father loves to talk.'

Gayle giggled, but not Janie. She pressed tighter against her mother. Susan circled her arm about the girl's thin shoulder. 'It's all right, sweetheart. Daddy's only doing business somewhere. He'll be with us soon.'

Slattery said, 'I'm having McPeck and Frank Shields ride back to Lovell and Red Lodge.' He glanced aside at the Conestoga and Steve Murfee riding toward them from the drag.

'You'll go into Yellowstone,' Susan Huffaker said. She stared ahead along the pass winding down through the low foothills. 'We'll be hours getting in with all these wagons.'

The six mules which drew the heavy freighter slowed to a halt. From the driver's seat Judy Fiske studied Slattery. 'What is it, Tom?' she called. She brushed loose strands of her black hair away from her forehead, her calm gray eyes serious. Lottie Wells, sitting next to her, did not speak. She was as dark-haired and finely shaped as Judy. Both women had deep-tanned skin that showed little dryness despite the months of trail-driving under the scorching sun. Lottie watched Steve Murfee draw in his buckskin. She listened while Slattery spoke to the cattlehand.

'I'm sending McPeck and Shields to check if Fred and Ian had to stop south of here,' he said. 'You and I will ride ahead into the town and see about the buyers. Gus Vierra's taking the chuck wagon in with Cookie. We'll pick up supplies while we're there.'

Murfee's leathery features hardened. 'They weren't with Gibson, Tom? Neither of them?' He saw how the two small Huffaker girls stayed close to their mother and immediately wished he hadn't asked.

'We'll go in,' Slattery repeated easily. He looked at the two women on the Conestoga's wide board seat. 'You stay with Sue. Maybe the girls can play in the back of your wagon.'

'Of course.' Judy smiled. Lottie moved aside to let the girls climb over the wagon side. 'We'll play a game,' she said. 'Janie and I will count the trees to the left of the pass, Gayle and Judy will count the trees to the right.'

The children remained beside their mother. Susan suddenly broke into laughter. 'Go ahead,' she told them, 'I'll count both sides and be judge. We'll see who wins when we get into the valley.'

12

'It's all right with you?' Gayle asked.

'Certainly it is. I'll want a few minutes alone with Daddy when he comes back anyway.' She laughed. 'I couldn't get a word in with you two here.'

Both laughing, the girls stepped from the carreta into the larger wagon. Susan waited for the Conestoga to draw ahead of her before she started her mules. Slattery and Murfee rode off past the big freighter. She knew the two men were as concerned as she was. Neither Ian nor Fred were the kind to not have word sent back to her about anything that might have happened. Ian, Ian, she thought. Tom had wanted another of the single men to ride ahead with Fred McDonald, but Ian had insisted. He'd have a chance to pick one of the best homesites, he had told her, by going in ahead of the trail drive.

Susan took a long, deep breath as she jiggled the reins to start the team. She felt like crying, but she couldn't because of the girls, She didn't want the best homesite in the valley. Right now she only wanted her husband with her where she knew he was alive and safe.

*   *   *

'You check with the sheriff,' Slattery told Murfee. 'If there was any trouble, he would know about it.'

Nodding,   the   tall   cowhand   studied

13

Yellowstone City. The four small ranches they had passed as they rode in had looked as dried up and dirt poor as the Gibson spread. The town was another thing. There were only five business buildings, all built at the intersections of four streets. The largest and oldest was a general store with a saloon attached. It was two-story, the windows above the long wide porch curtained, used either as living quarters for the storekeeper or to hire out. The smaller structures were built of wood so newly cut the boards showed hardly any seasoning. The bank and sheriff's office stood directly across from the store, side by side in the same building. A large sign, U.S. LAND OFFICE, painted in high black letters, filled the entire false front diagonally opposite the blacksmith and harness shop. The homes of Yellowstone City were built about one-hundred yards behind the store. The three men and lone woman on the porches and walks showed momentary interest in the two riders, then continued with their business.

'If Fred and Ian were here,' Murfee said, 'they'd've showed. I don't like it, Tom. I'll come into the land office with you.'

'Get the sheriff. I want him in there too.' Slattery shifted in the saddle, motioning behind them to Augustin Vierra and Walter Cook in the canvas-topped chuck wagon. 'Buy everything you'll need,' he called. 'We'll try to get over and help you load.'

14

Slattery rode ahead and crossed the wide, dusty intersection as Murfee turned toward the jail hitchrail. Slattery's mouth was dry. He spat, tasting the ever-present bitterness of alkali they had all lived with the past three months. The valley between Gibson's and the Calligan had been almost as burnt and dead as the bunch grass they had kept the herd alive on, but he could see now that Fred McDonald had really known the promise of this land. Green grass stretched from the far side of the river bank across the miles of rolling range between the town and the high granite snow-patched peaks. He could see only three ranches off in the distance, each a small spread. Acres and acres of virgin land along the banks of the Calligan's curved sweep, clear to the dark-shaded pine or the timberline, waited for the Texans to build homes and develop its potential.

The land office was one long room with a high, saloonlike counter that ran its entire length. The clerk sat at the desk in the near corner. He glanced up when Slattery entered, then laid down his pencil and stood. He was almost as tall as Slattery, and was neatly dressed in black trousers, a blue string tie dangling from the buttoned collar of his white shirt. He drew a black slim cheroot from between his lips, exhaling the smoke toward the rear door.

'Yes, sir,' he said. 'Can I help you?'

15

Slattery introduced himself and began to ask about McDonald and Huffaker. The clerk interrupted. He was grinning now, openly happy the herd had arrived. 'We thought you'd be in earlier,' he said in a loud voice. 'I'd been looking for someone from your crew to reach town a couple weeks ago. I wanted time to get things ready for you.'

'Two of our men did come,' said Slattery. 'They rode ahead of our herd on the eighteenth.'

The clerk had raised the slim Mexican cigar to his mouth. He lowered it and leaned forward against the counter. 'They didn't come, Mr. Slattery. No one came.' His stare switched to the front door.

Steve Murfee stepped inside with a lawman about his own age, but the resemblance ended there. The sheriff was short and stocky, with tremendous arms and shoulders that bulged the faded blue workshirt that held his shiny silver star.

The government land clerk opened the gate in the counter and stepped out. 'Ben,' he said to the sheriff, 'that Texan we expected did head here. Two of them did, Mr. Slattery says. They never got to me.'

Ben Shepperd nodded. He glanced from Slattery to Murfee. 'Two of them?' he repeated. His wide, square jaw tightened and he brushed one big hand across his jowls. 'Ketchuck here was lookin' for your man.

16

More than a week ago he told me to keep a lookout.' He shook his head from side to side. 'No stranger's been in this town. Let alone two of them.'

'I'd prepared everything I could, Mr. Slattery,' said Donald Ketchuck. He pointed to the large black ink drawing which showed the entire length and breadth of Calligan Valley. Squares were shaded in with pencil where ranches were already settled. Everything else was left open and white, with dotted lines to define the acreage allowed for purchase by government order. 'If one of you want to go with Sheriff Shepperd, I'll be glad to explain the regulations on this.'

Slattery did not answer. He stared through the window and across the quiet square. Cook had left the wagon at the store rail. Augustin Vierra was already loading a wooden boxful of supplies onto the tailgate.

'Thanks, Mr. Ketchuck,' Slattery said. 'We'll have our people come in.'

Ketchuck said, 'Fine. I'll be here. I'll keep the office open tonight.' He gazed past the window. 'I hope you find your men.' His stare switched to the sheriff.

'I'll go out with you,' Shepperd told Slattery. 'There's plenty that could have happened 'tween here and where your men left your herd.'

'I've sent men looking, Sheriff.' Slattery gripped the doorknob, then paused. 'How

17

about the storekeeper or blacksmith? Any of them done any traveling the past couple of weeks?'

'No, not that I know . . . I'm not sure though.' Shepperd turned to the clerk. 'Myron Blumberg went after that piano for Goodlove. How long ago?'

'That piano?' Ketchuck repeated. 'I'd say closer to two weeks ago.'

The lawman nodded his blocky head. 'I'll go over to the grocery with you,' he told Slattery. 'See what Myron knows.' He walked outside in front of Murfee and Slattery.

Ketchuck stood at the counter and watched the three until they were almost across the intersection of Four Corners. He flicked the ashes from the cheroot onto the unpainted pine floor. Then he put the cigar between his lips and returned to his desk.

The door to the back room opened and a tall, thin man dressed in cowhand's clothing started into the office. Ketchuck swung around. 'Don't come in here, you fool,' the clerk snapped. 'They're not even to the store yet.'

The man's lean, muscular body did not halt. 'You sonofabitch,' he snapped, his words grating as sharply as Ketchuck's had. 'Watch your talk. You hear that?' He stopped with his face close to the clerk. His mouth was thin and cunning, his eyes watchful, tight—not the eyes of a working cattlehand.

18

The two men who followed him were as openly hostile. Neither was more than twenty. Like their leader, they did not wear guns. The older had a sneer on his face that twisted his pencil-line mustache. The other was red-haired and beardless. Unconsciously his left hand brushed across his pants leg exactly where a thonged-down sixgun would hang.

'Your job's to get something started in the street,' Ketchuck said. He had not edged away an inch from the trio. 'If you're seen in here, you'll answer to Goodlove.'

'We'll be out there,' the leader said. 'You just keep that tongue of yours civil.'

The second man's mustache curled into a grin. 'We give this pencil-pusher a quick lesson, Dancer?' His grin included the redhead. 'What say, Calem?' The three shifted their stances.

Ketchuck backed from the desk, one step, then another, toward the counter. 'Damn it, they'll be gone. You'll miss your chance. I don't want you to miss.'

'That's all right,' Jim Dancer said. 'You just choose your words more careful.' He began to turn.

Ketchuck said, 'Do it right this time. No mistakes like with the other two. They've got Shepperd and half their trail crew looking for them. You know what Goodlove wants.'

'We know what we do, clerk,' said Dancer. 'The boss'll see we were right with that pair.

Well do right here, too.' Ketchuck opened his mouth to speak, then shut it as fast when Dancer's big right fist came up.

'You watch out that window.' Dancer's voice was calm and hard and sure. 'You'll see we do it just like the boss wants.'

CHAPTER THREE

Myron Blumberg shook his head. 'I didn't go south that day,' he said. 'As soon as I was through the pass, I drove straight east to Bozeman. I didn't see anyone. I'm sorry, but that's all I can tell you.'

'Ralph Goodlove was in that day, wasn't he?' Sheriff Shepperd asked. 'How far did he ride with you?'

The small, thin storekeeper was silent, soberly thoughtful before he answered. He was one of the quietest and most orderly men in Yellowstone City, and one of the most respected. The neat, clean way his counters and shelves were stocked with every item from bandannas to men's suits and women's calico dresses, was all part of his person. And this contributed to his thriving business. Shepperd knew from the Town Board meetings that the storekeeper always gave thought to whatever he said. Blumberg never raised his voice in threats or demands. He stood for what he believed in, and he believed in the future of Calligan Valley. He'd given generous credit to the drought-poor ranchers who needed it. This and the love he'd had for his dead wife and daughter were known by everyone. Shepperd had complete trust and confidence in him. He'd never doubted a word Myron Blumberg said, nor what he told them now.

'Mr. Goodlove rode as far as Gibson's with me. Jim Dancer and Calem Torrey were with him.' He looked at Slattery. 'If I didn't see your two men, I doubt they did. They didn't ride any further than Gibson's'.

Slattery nodded. He said to Shepperd, 'I'd like to talk to them anyway.'

The lawman walked to the swinging doors which separated the store from the saloon. He stared over the batwings, then again at the men. 'None of them is in there.'

'Mr. Goodlove could be at Churchill's house,' the storekeeper offered. He moved a few steps along the counter to lift a wooden box and hold it for Augustin Vierra to carry out to the wagon. The Mexican hefted it onto his right shoulder.

'These three are the last Cookie ordered,' he told Slattery. 'Do you want us to stay in town and help you look?'

'No, you both head back,' Slattery said. 'Steve and I will stay in and see what we can learn.'

Sheriff Ben Shepperd said, 'I'll go out to

21

Churchill's house and ask Mr. Goodlove to come in.'

'We'll go with you,' Slattery said.

'No, its just outback here. Churchill's been laid up, and the fewer people who visit him, the better.' He headed toward the store's stockroom door at the rear of the long wide room.

Cook had pushed past the screen door and stopped to speak to Augustin Vierra. Slattery realized there was nothing more he could learn until the lawman returned with the man named Goodlove. He glanced at the two remaining boxes piled high with sacks of flour and tins of food and the other items Cook had bought. 'Cookie, this all you need?' he questioned. 'They'll be good and hungry once the herd's in.'

'Yep. That's 'bout all,' Cook answered. He left Augustin Vierra and walked toward the rear counter.

Vierra pulled open the screen door and stepped out onto the porch. He wanted to stay in town and help find out what had become of Fred McDonald and Ian. Two such responsible men do not simply vanish. Even before they reached this valley, it seems, they had vanished. He felt, too, that Thomãs Slattery realized the truth in this. Yet he had been with Thomãs long enough to know the trail boss would stay right here until he learned every fact. This was no ordinary trail drive and

Thomãs was no ordinary leader. The families had driven their cattle from Texas after five years of drought. They believed in this new wide-open land, in its promise, in the hope of new lives. The lack of rain here had not been expected, but still it was not as bad as the barren, sun-scorched flats around San Saba.

Vierra thanked the trail drive for bringing Slattery to his town of Estancia along the Rio Bravo. He had been taken along with the Texan, as their equal, and he too had a new life to look forward to and plan. He was thinking of this, hardly noting the burning heat of the sun while he set the heavy box atop the others he and Wally Cook had put into the chuck wagon. He heard the slow, steady clopping of horses' hoofs approach him from the square, but he did not turn or give attention to the sound.

'Hey! You, Mex!' a voice called sharply. 'What you doin' at that wagon, Mex?'

Vierra heard the insult in the man's tone. He had heard it often enough where he'd been born. He held down the quick anger that always came to him at times like this. He backed from the tailgate, intending to return to the store.

'Mex! Damn you! You look here!' The rider on a bay horse spurred his animal between Vierra and the bottom porch step. He was young and rawboned and tall in the saddle. The rider to his left was redheaded. He

23

grinned widely. 'Hold him!' he shouted. 'Hold him, Dancer!'

Dancer wheeled his bay's rump, blocking the space between the hitchrails. 'You don't belong in this town, Mex-boy!' he snapped. 'Git up in that wagon and drive.'

'I have not finished loading,' Vierra answered. He caught sight of Cook watching from the doorway above Dancer, then he heard the sound of a rope swishing through the air.

The rope, thrown by a third, mustached rider behind Vierra, slipped over Vierra's shoulders. The noose was pulled snug, pinning his arms to his sides. He was jerked and flung backwards, stumbling to stay on his feet.

'You got him! Throw him, Waco,' the redhead cried. Dancer kneed the bay closer and closer to the man struggling to gain his foothold. Vierra tried to reach the tightened cope with his hands, but the mustached rider jerked harder and threw him to the ground.

The redhead screamed in laughter. Dancer's bay's hoofs kicked the dust close to Vierra's legs. Vierra rolled over once, then again, to get clear of the horses. He was on his hands and knees trying to push himself erect. His sombrero was torn from his head and sent rolling under the wagon. Vierra stared up at the mustached face, seeing the rider's eyes shine in his bony head.

'Drag him!' the redhead laughed. 'He's

smart. He won't git! Drag the bastard!'

Vierra, struggling to his feet, was jerked down again. His face smashed the earth, the dust gagged him. He knew he was going to be dragged. He could feel the rope strain and pull and the sand begin to scrape against his stomach, chest, and legs. He held his breath so the dust wouldn't choke him. Then from far off he heard Slattery's voice.

'Stop that! Stop that horse or I'll drill you right out of that saddle!'

CHAPTER FOUR

The instant Cook had yelled about what was happening in the street, Slattery had run for the porch, his .44 Colt in his hand. He aimed the muzzle directly at Waco Jones' chest.

'Don't let your horse swing,' he snapped. 'Hold it! Now, Mister!' He was alongside Dancer's bay, taking a stride to the right to pass wide of the horsemen.

Behind Dancer, Steve Murfee shouted as loudly as Slattery had. 'Any one of you move in on him, I'll cut him down! Any one!' The click of his sixgun cocking was as clear as a gunshot in the sudden silence.

Waco stopped his sorrel mare. He had seen hard, dangerous men before. He had helped bury others who had been foolish enough to push them too far. He hadn't figured on men like these. The other two cowhands who had showed up ahead of this crew had been so easy to handle. Not these two.

'That's it,' Slattery ordered. 'Slack up on the rope! Drop it! Now!'

The lariat slipped from Waco's fingers. His eyes flicked to Dancer who still laughed while he looked down at Slattery. There was a wicked gleam of pleasure on Dancer's face, not one bit of worry.

'Hell, man,' Dancer said, catching his breath from laughing. 'We was jest funnin'! This Mex here, he jest don't belong!'

'He would make ten of you,' Slattery snapped. 'Scum like you won't stand up to a man alone. None of you.'

Dancer's smile faded. 'You got a gun, Mister. You put away that gun.'

Vierra had pushed himself up onto his feet. He coughed and spat dust while he struggled to throw the loop off his shoulders. Steve Murfee holstered his sixgun. He stepped toward Dancer. 'I'm not holdin' a gun on you,' he said.

Dancer kicked the bay forward and smashed the horse's side into the cattlehand, knocking Murfee backwards so his head and spine were slammed viciously against a wheel of the chuck wagon. The bay mare continued its charge straight at Slattery. Dancer crouched in the saddle. One of his arms reached out to knock the Colt from Slattery's hand.

Slattery sidestepped. He caught hold of the outstretched hand, locked his fingers about the wrist, and pulled. Dancer, off balance, could not stay in the saddle. He was hurled to the ground, landing on the left side of his head and shoulder. He lay there dazed, sprawled out on his back.

Waco Jones and the redhead had not moved, everything had happened so fast. Vierra straightened and spat again. His stance was sure while he looked up at Jones and waited for the rider to try to help Dancer. Steve Murfee stepped away from the wagon toward the redhead's horse. His mind still hazy, his eyes burning, Dancer slowly sat in the dust. Blood oozed from his nose and scraped face. He tried to stand, but rolled onto his left side. He pushed himself onto one knee, his vision clearer now. He crouched, ready to tackle Slattery.

'Go ahead,' Slattery invited coldly. 'Give me a chance.' He jammed his Colt down under the waistband of his jeans and beckoned the man toward him.

'Don't move! Dancer!'

The shouted words were loud, demanding. Dancer froze. Slattery glanced at the two men who had shoved past the screen door with Sheriff Ben Shepperd. The man who had called the order was tall and well-dressed, his stance on the top porch step as tight and

27

controlled as the authority in his voice.

'You wanted to play,' Slattery said to Dancer. He beckoned with one hand. 'Try me.'

'All three of you,' Murfee added, edging closer to Vierra. 'All three.'

'They'll stay right where they are,' the tall, finely-dressed man with Sheriff Shepperd said coming down the stairs. He stared from Jones to the redhead and Dancer. 'What were you men trying to do?'

'We was just funnin', Mr. Goodlove,' Dancer said. He spat a mouthful of blood and dust, then slowly stood.

'They were going to drag this man,' Slattery said. 'You see the rope, Mister. That's all you've got to see.'

'Yes, I see it, and I regret it.' Ralph Goodlove halted between Slattery and Dancer. Physically, Goodlove was impressive, handsome, with a big, well-padded body, graying hair and a tanned complexion that showed as much attention was given to his person as to his expensive black Stetson and tailor-made gray suit and white shirt. He clearly was not a man who had earned his wealth and position through a lifetime of cattle-handling. There was something strong about him, standing straight and tall, his eyes glued to his cowhands. 'I allow the three of you to visit town and this is what happens? Well, it won't happen again.'

'Listen, Mr. Goodlove,' Dancer began. 'We

do things like this—'

'Not while you work for me,' Goodlove snapped. 'You do nothing which will degrade another man. Nothing, do you hear?'

The redheaded rider shifted uncomfortably in his saddle. 'Look, Boss, he's only a Mex.'

'He's a man.' The voice grew louder, demanding. 'I came into this valley to run a business. Not to get hate from my neighbors.' He allowed his glance to include Slattery and the sheriff. 'These people are settling in this valley, the same as myself. We need them. I don't care what kind they are. No one who works for me does one thing to hurt a good relationship.' To the lawman he said, 'If this man wants to prefer charges, Sheriff Shepperd, you do your duty.'

Shepperd looked at Augustin Vierra. 'You say the word.'

The Mexican shook his head. 'They did me no harm,' he said. His stare shifted to the three cowhands. 'This will not happen again. It will not.'

'You can bet on that.' Steve Murfee picked up the noose of the lariat that lay in the roadway. He coiled it while he walked close to Waco Jones' horse. 'You try that again, you'll learn it ain't no fun to be dragged.'

Jones took the rope. Dancer snorted, 'Hell, Mr. Goodlove. We weren't lookin' for real trouble. You said we don't wear guns in town, we don't.' He nodded at Vierra's holstered

29

Remington .32, and at Slattery and Murfee. 'We ain't foolish enough to go up against trail hands fresh in from a drive. Not when they're packin' and we're not.' He turned his head and his glance scanned thirty or more people who had come out onto the walks and porches. Three young boys stood in an alleyway which led to the cluster of homes. 'We been workin' for Mr. Goodlove a year now. People in this town know we don't push trouble.'

'And you won't in the future,' Goodlove told the trio. 'Not if you want to keep your jobs.' He motioned in the direction of the residential section. 'Go down to Churchill's. I'll have more to say to you when I get there.'

Without another word the three cowhands walked their horses through the square. Cook and Myron Blumberg, who had watched from the store porch, carried the boxes they had been holding down the stairs and over to the wagon. Slattery studied the faces of the people in the streets. Everyone, the children included, seemed to be very shocked and disturbed by what had happened. A few of the men eyed Augustin Vierra closely, as though he could be the one to blame. Slattery said to Vierra, 'You and Cookie start back. Tell Weaver we'll bed the herd out where it is till each man gets to visit the land office. Have Lute push the remuda across the river so we don't use too much grass on either side.'

'What about Señora Huffaker?' Vierra

asked. 'She will have questions.'

'I'll be out soon. Tell her . . . I'll talk to her when I get back.'

'Si,' the Mexican said. He raised his booted foot onto the step plate and swung up onto the seat alongside Cook.

Goodlove said to Slattery, 'The sheriff asked me about two of your men who were supposed to have come into our valley. I'm sorry, Mr. Slattery. The day in question, I saw no strangers.' His voice was intently polite and still held a trace of the embarrassment that his cowhands had caused him. Only the inflection had changed. Where his sharpness had shown he had treated Dancer, Jones, and Torrey as subordinates, his tone to Slattery was that of equal talking to equal. 'I wish I could help you more.'

'You don't remember seeing anyone?' Slattery said. 'How about someone from this town, or the valley, who was out that way?'

Goodlove shook his head thoughtfully. Ben Shepperd said, 'You figure something happened to them, Slattery? We ain't had a bushwackin' since this valley's been settled. We ain't had any trouble.' He motioned to the storekeeper on the porch steps. 'You'll back me on that, Myron. This was the first trouble we've had.'

'Yes,' Blumberg answered. 'Mr. Slattery, I have customers who come in from beyond the pass. I'll ask them if they have seen your men.'

31

'Thanks,' Slattery told him. 'Sheriff, I'll keep in touch with you.' He turned with Steve Murfee to cross the intersection toward his black gelding.

Ralph Goodlove walked hurriedly to Slattery's side. 'I don't like to talk business, Mr. Slattery, with the problem you have. But I'm interested in buying some of the Longhorns you've brought here.'

'We're going to sell a portion of the herd,' Slattery told him. 'Soon as our families know where they'll settle. Fred McDonald said the other ranchers were willing to buy. We'll let you know.'

'Well, that's just it,' Goodlove moved at the same pace as Slattery, his tone and expression dead serious. 'You saw Gibson's ranch, and that he's lost most of his stock. This summer drought has hurt me and the other ranchers too. What they can't buy, I'll take off your hands.'

'I'll have to talk with the other men about what they intend to sell.'

'Fine. Fine. You do that,' Goodlove smiled, showing his even set of very white teeth. His voice grew quieter. 'I'll take the entire forty-five-hundred head. Of course, with the summer hitting so hard, and the grass fires, I'll have to ask a cut in price.'

'Oh?' Slattery was annoyed to realize exactly why the rancher had kept after him. The smooth talk and effort at charm had taken him in, but not anymore.

'We don't have that many cows,' he said flatly. 'We sold close to a thousand head in Dodge for money to pay for land. Each rancher plans to hold a stocking herd of his own. We'll let you know what we can sell.'

They had reached the land office hitchrail. Murfee was untying his buckskin at the jail. Slattery untied King and looked beyond the intersection. The chuck wagon had crossed the log bridge that spanned the river, and Vierra and Cook were out of sight behind the cottonwoods and willows that lined the high bank. Overhead, the noonday sun was a solid gold disk in the cloudless sky. The day was beautiful, peaceful, but the hint of smoke in the air, the trouble the Goodlove riders had made, even the cagey game the rancher tried to play with him, gave the silence of the town and valley a lie. 'We'll let you know,' Slattery repeated.

'But I planned on buying a sizable herd,' Goodlove said. 'I can give you a better price than anyone in the valley.'

'You'll be given the same deal as every other rancher, Mr. Goodlove,' Slattery said. 'I have a woman and her two children to talk to.' He stepped into the stirrup, pulled himself into the saddle, and swung the black to meet Steve Murfee.

Ralph Goodlove stood alone in the street, watching the two riders head east away from

Four Corners. Goodlove swore to himself. He had not known about the cattle sell in Dodge, hadn't planned on the Texans having their own money with them. He did not realise that Slattery was like he was earlier, he wouldn't have the time to drag out what he intended, not with a strong man leading the bloc of new homesteaders. Damn it, he thought, and then he calmed. Things had gone wrong before. He'd had to act fast and cover up after the way Dancer and Jones had handled the other two Texans. Such a stupid senseless thing to do . . . but he'd covered that. He'd handle this problem just as well.

The land office door squeaked as it opened behind him. Ketchuck's footfall scuffed on the porch boards. The government agent stepped down beside Goodlove.

'That was a fine show,' Ketchuck chuckled. 'It won't hurt Dancer to be cut down to size. He won't act so quick on his own again.'

'He won't. None. of you will,' Goodlove said. To anyone watching the two men, they simply spoke quietly, but the tight calm in Goodlove's voice wiped the smile from Ketchuck's lips. 'Those ranchers will have cash for their land. Make certain every deed is written according to strict law. Don't make any mistakes.'

'I won't. This Slattery—'

'I'll handle Slattery. You just make certain the government inspectors can't pick us up on

34

even the slightest irregularity.'

'There won't be a chance,' Ketchuck said. He glanced toward Slattery and Murfee walking their horses across the log bridge. 'I'd have a federal offense against me. Not one of those hayshakers will have reason to complain to Slattery.'

Ralph Goodlove nodded without speaking. He drew a gold case from his coat pocket. The cigarettes inside were already rolled, each the same length and size. He lit one, drew in a lungful of smoke, and slowly exhaled. There wasn't a hint of doubt in his tone.

'Dancer has damn good reason to act next time he's pushed,' he said. 'I promise you, we won't be bothered by Slattery.'

CHAPTER FIVE

'That's all anyone knows, Sue,' Tom Slattery said. 'As far as I can tell, neither Fred nor Ian reached this valley. I've sent Lonnie Day and Alf Flynn to catch up with McPeck and Shields and check every mile of the trail into the valley.'

Susan Huffaker did not answer. She stared toward the cluster of wagons where Judy Fiske had stayed with her two little girls. Most of the other children crowded around the chuck wagon. Walter Cook had started the fire, and the boys and girls laughed and chattered while they helped Augustin Vierra rig a canvas roof to shade Cookie's work table. One group of boys drove four poles into the sandy ground, while others, boys and girls, helped unroll the canvas so it could be lifted, pulled taut and tied over the pole tops. The news about Ian and Fred had been told to all of the adults, but she didn't want her girls to know. Not yet, not until they were absolutely certain. Finally, she nodded. 'Thank you, Tom.' Her tired, lined face did not relax. 'I'll wait right here.'

'Sue, I never thought anything like this could happen,' Slattery said. 'The drive's been so easy since we left Dodge.'

'Ian asked to go,' she answered. 'Tom, I know you told him you'd rather send one of the single men.' She shook her head as she scanned the wide valley floor to the thick brush and timber that screened the water. 'For this? It isn't worth it. Not for this.'

Slattery glanced from the chuck wagon to the horses which had been staked out to graze a half mile behind the wagons so they would not raise dust close to the campsite. The cattle watered near the pass and fed on the tall, lush grass along the river bank. The Texas cowmen had stayed away from the Huffaker carreta while Slattery spoke to Ian's wife. Their women prepared their own meals for their own families, yet they kept glancing at the wagon, wanting to come over and console

Susan. The men grouped together and talked. Now and then one of them kicked at the gray cracked earth or squinted into the sun's brassy glare, disappointed at traveling so far just to find they had to face another drought. The four riders who had stayed with the herd did not bother to haze back the tail-switching, fly-stomping steers which tried to cross the sparkling white sandbars to the opposite bank. The earth was just as parched beyond drinking distance on that side. The cattle would straggle back long before dust.

'This has been an extra bad summer for them too,' Slattery said. 'Clear down to the Panhandle it's been like this, Susan. The fall rains should—'

'I don't care about the fall rains. Not if Ian isn't here.' She stood from the wagon seat, her body held straight and firm. 'The girls will be hungry. I'll get their food ready.'

Slattery took her arm and helped her down. 'We'll find out,' he said.

Susan simply said, 'It's the children. I know something has happened. I feel it. But I don't know what to do or to say to the children.' She took a wooden water bucket from the tailgate and moved slowly toward Judy Fiske's Conestoga wagon.

Slattery watched her. He wished he could help her more, that he could give her some hope. He couldn't lie about Ian and McDonald. He couldn't lie about the

37

condition of the land. The men and women and children who had made the long trail drive had left a burned-out range and had believed in the promise of something better ahead of them. What they had gained was better than the flats of San Saba, but a herd this size would finish off the good grass in short order. 'The worst summer we've had in twenty years,' Gibson had told him . . . The promise they all wanted to believe in could still be here if rain came. They would have to last it out . . .

'Tom,' a voice said behind Slattery.

Mal Weaver, followed by three other men, approached him. The stubby, whiskered cowman had hung back until Susan reached the Conestoga. Weaver watched Susan lift her two daughters from the freighter and lead them toward the river to get water.

'She's takin' it good,' Weaver said. 'I don't know how my woman'd take somethin like that.' He shook his head. 'Tom, I rode out along the river eight, maybe ten miles. There's better graze land the further in you go. If Sue wants, I'll take her in and get the paperwork started for her on some prime bottomland.'

'I'd like to go in too,' Ed Anderson said. 'The sooner we get our boundaries set, the sooner we c'n start buildin'.' He was lanky and angular and prematurely gray for thirty-eight. He had a wife and six children to think of, and Slattery could see he considered them while he spoke. 'I didn't get much out of the Dodge sell.

I'd like to start cuttin' tomorrow, soon as I have an idea where I'll build.'

'I would too,' said Byron Cullen. 'I reckon I'll hold most of my stockers. But I've got some fours and long threes I can market.'

'We might have to hold off on that.' Slattery told them about his talk with Goodlove. He could read the change in Cullen's leathery features before he finished.

'I didn't sell in Dodge because I thought we'd get a higher price here,' Cullen told him. 'I need money in hand to buy land.'

'We'll see about bank loans,' Slattery said.

'How, with stock that won't bring a fair price? Tom, I joined up because I figured I'd do better for my woman and younguns. I would've at least had land and a roof over our heads on the Llano.' He looked at Weaver. 'I told Hanna I'd take the whole family into that town with me. You think you c'n talk Nancy into waitin' until we learn how things stand at the bank?'

Weaver stared toward his wagon. His wife and their small daughter had finished their meal. They had washed and dried everything, and both his family and Cullen's wife and four children were inside their wagons with the flaps pulled down while they dressed to go into the town.

Weaver shook his head. 'I don't know. I promised.'

'Mal, I don't want Hanna to see if I'm

39

refused a loan,' Cullen said. 'I'll need time to decide.'

Slattery said, 'Take your families in, both of you. I've got two hundred head I can put up for you. I'll go into the bank with you.'

'Wal, sure, I'll get them,' Cullen said. 'I appreciate this, Tom.' He grinned and with Weaver and the other men started toward the wagons. Near the river Susan Huffaker stood talking quietly to her two small blond-haired girls. Slattery wanted to go to them, to somehow give them hope their husband and father was safe. He didn't do that, nor did he stop for a few words with Judy Fiske. Judy would be driving into town with the families and he would have time to see her then. He had to check on the remuda and herd, to make certain no problem could come up while he was away. He wanted to speak to Lute Canby, who was the last man to talk with Ian and Fred before they left the herd to ride north. He wanted to see if there was anything at all, just one small fact or thought or idea that might tell him what could have happened to the two men.

* * *

Myron Blumberg tried to find someone who knew something about what had happened to Ian Huffaker and Fred McDonald. Blumberg's store had been the center of interest in

40

Yellowstone City ever since the trouble had taken place outside in the street. The news of what had happened had been told to everyone who came into town, and eventually each person, man and woman and child, ended up talking and listening to Myron.

The roping of Vierra, and Slattery's facing down of Goodlove's three riders was the first trouble ever to happen right out on Four Corners. But trouble was no stranger to Myron. He had once had a wife and a baby son, and he had lost both of them in childbirth when he was a very, very young man. It seemed so long ago, it made him feel older than sixty-two, yet it was still so fresh in his mind he remembered it as though it was yesterday, and the hurt of the loss was always with him.

He had left Kansas City not long after he had buried his wife and son. He lived for a while in Wichita and later in Omaha. He had come up into the Montana Territory when he heard that gold strikes had been made in Grasshopper Creek, Bannock, and the Last Chance. He had seen too much violence, the worst in Alder Gulch and during the wild, free days of Virginia City. He had lived through the times of the vigilante law, when short work was made of men like George Ives and Boone Helm and Henry Plummer. He had seen what the insane drives for money and power could do to men. When he had first come into

41

Calligan Valley six years ago, he had had his own vision of what life could be like. He had found the peace he had always wanted. It was not a complete feeling, because he always lived with his sense of loss. But it was a proper peace.

Until today.

Myron kept to himself his own beliefs about the real reason behind the trouble Ralph Goodlove's riders had caused with Slattery's cowhands, the deep hate he had seen in the faces of Dancer, Jones, and Torrey, and his own knowledge from experience that a man like Slattery would never back down a step from what he knew was right. To the people who wanted to know about the trouble, he simply repeated what he had witnessed. He also repeated the questions Slattery had asked him concerning the two men who had ridden out ahead of the cattle drive and who were supposed to have reached Yellowstone City six days earlier.

No one showed much interest in the two missing men until Cal Teller arrived at the store just after two o'clock that afternoon. Cal drummed pots and pans all through the Territory. He came into Blumberg's store at the end of each month. He had been due in that morning, but he had changed his route to visit the Webster ranch in the southwest corner of the valley. Webster's wife had burned a frying pan clear through. She had been after

Cal to replace it since the last winter. Cal had gone straight to Webster's to deliver the new pan before he rode into town.

Cal listened to Myron's account of the trouble, but did not speak until the storekeeper mentioned the two missing riders. 'You said two of them?' he asked. 'And they haven't been seen between here and Lovell?'

'That's what Mr. Slattery told me,' Myron said.

Cal's round, friendly face was thoughtful. 'One was kinda big and red-faced? The other an older cowpuncher?' When Myron answered that he did not know either man, the drummer went on, 'I bumped into two riders 'bout a week ago, near the Big Horn. One had a funny name I never heard before.'

'Ian?' said Myron Blumberg. 'Ian Huffaker?'

Teller nodded. 'Yes. That's it. Sounded like a woman's name when his friend spoke to him.' He shook his head. 'Funny thing. I saw Jim Dancer the next morning too. He passed my rig, way off.'

'You're sure it was Dancer?' Myron questioned. 'You're sure you saw him out of the valley?'

The drummer nodded. 'I couldn't miss Dancer's big bay horse. He was pretty far off, but it was him.'

Two homesteaders' wives waited at the dry goods counter, but Myron forgot about them.

43

He took hold of the drummer's arm and started to hurry him toward the door.

'Hey, hey, Myron!' Cal complained. 'I came here to sell, not to go runnin' off.'

'We'll come back and do business,' the storekeeper told him. 'You tell Ben Shepperd what you told me. Then we'll come back.'

He pushed open the screen door and made the drummer move ahead of him across the porch and down the steps into the blistering daylight heat. The slight afternoon breeze gave no relief from the sun and smelled of smoke. It was an acrid odor that made Myron's nostrils smart and told him that grass and pine were burning on the far side of the mountains. The loss in timber would hurt, but the fires would eventually be put out, winter would come, and the next spring new grass and timber would grow again. The same was not true about a man who was knifed or shot. And Myron Blumberg believed he knew what had happened to the two riders from Slattery's trail drive.

*   *   *

Tom Slattery pulled the brim of his flat-crowned hat down lower over his eyes. He had held King close to the Weaver wagon while he spoke with Mal and Nancy Weaver and Judy Fiske on the driver's seat alongside them. Weaver's daughter and two other children who

44

had been piled into the back of the vehicle talked and laughed among themselves as the iron-rimmed wheels rumbled over the thick logs of the bridge. Slattery heard Nancy Weaver say, 'Oh, we'll have enough time,' but the words hardly registered with him. Three men had appeared from the jail doorway. One was the sheriff, the second was Blumberg who ran the general store. Slattery had never seen the third man before.

Along the roadway which led into Four Corners, the wide shadows lengthened as the sun lowered toward the southwest, but the furnacelike heat did not dampen the spirits of the settlers. They had traveled more than twelve-hundred long, tiresome, hard miles. Nothing, not the sepia dust kicked up in small bursts by the mules' hoofs, nor the constant heady smelt of fire smoke, interfered with their first look at their new town. It was range grass and yellow pine that burned, Slattery thought judging from the acrid smell of the breeze. The fires were outside the valley, off toward the Gallatin and Madison Mountains. A bluish haze hung over the northern pass, yet somehow even the presence of smoke failed to take away from the beauty of the green and brown grass that stretched the full length of the winding sweep of the Calligan River.

'The land will cost more the other side of town,' Judy Fiske said. She looked at Slattery, waiting for him to answer. When he only

45

stared ahead, she repeated her thoughts. 'Land will cost more the farther out we go, Tom.'

Slattery nodded. 'Yes. It will.' Sheriff Shepperd, the storekeeper, and the third man had halted in the roadway and watched the wagons coming in.

'Tom, you're not listening,' Judy said. She sat straight, her face serious. She seemed cool and comfortable. Her long black hair was drawn away from her forehead, pulled back and tied with a blue ribbon along her neck. He hadn't given her his full attention. His mind had been on so many other things. They'd never actually made plans together, but it was understood by everyone she was his woman . . . He shifted his eyes from the men and looked at her.

'That is the best place to settle,' he told her. 'Plenty of water and grass. The windbreaks will give some shelter from storms. What I hear about Montana winters, we'll be snowed in often enough even if the wind holds down.'

Judy smiled. 'I don't care about that. In my own home, with my own family.'

Steve Murfee had ridden ahead from the second wagon. He slowed alongside Slattery's black gelding. Augustin Vierra rode directly behind the cattlehand. He drew in abreast of Murfee.

'Shepperd's wavin' to you,' Murfee said to Slattery. 'What do you figure?'

Slattery glanced at Weaver. 'Tie up with the others near the land office, Mal,' he said. 'There'll be enough time for each man to talk to the agent, and for the women to shop around. Pass the word the last wagon should be ready to leave at sunset.'

Judy said, 'Tom, aren't you going to stay with us? I thought . . .'

'I'll talk to the sheriff, then I'll meet you,' Slattery answered. 'You and the other women will want to spend some time at the store. I'll find you.' He turned King toward the jail.

Sheriff Ben Shepperd met them before they reached the hitchrails and spoke before they stopped their horses. 'We think we've learned something about your two men,' he said. Slattery, Murfee, and Vierra sat without moving until he finished telling them what Cal Teller had seen. Murfee stared angrily toward the town's residential section and swung down from the saddle. 'Dancer went into one of the houses,' he snapped. 'I'll see if he's still there.' He dropped his right hand and adjusted the hang of his holstered sixgun.

'No, you won't,' Shepperd said. 'Anythin' that's done, is done legal. All the way.'

Murfee's expression had not changed. He was going to snap an answer, but Slattery spoke first. 'You're sure you saw Dancer?' he asked the heavy-set drummer.

'It was his horse. He was off in the distance, but I know it was his big bay horse.' He

47

nodded to Blumberg. 'I told Myron exactly what I saw. One of the two men I met was named Ian. That's dead truth.'

Murfee watched while Slattery and Vierra dismounted. Slattery glanced up and down the roadway, noting that only a few of Yellowstone City's citizens had come out of the buildings to see the wagons and the new people who would become a part of their town. Two men stood on the bank porch. Three women and a boy were on the steps of the general store. Slattery had expected that the government land agent would open his office door and welcome the settlers who wanted to buy land, yet the office door stayed closed.

'You'll come with us to face Dancer?' Slattery asked Teller.

Teller's round face became worried. 'Look, I do business in this valley.'

'You'll come,' Murfee said flatly. 'There's enough of us to back you.'

Teller hesitated. Slattery said to Ben Shepperd, 'Will you swear us in as deputies? Mr. Teller has nothing to be afraid of as long as he's backed by the law.'

Shepperd looked directly into Teller's eyes. 'All you're doin' is sayin' Dancer was out of the valley when you met those men. You aren't accusin' him of anything.' He turned to Slattery. 'You realize that? We talk to Dancer, we only talk. No gunplay.'

'You'll swear us in?' Slattery asked.

48

Shepperd shook his head. 'No, I won't. And you won't wear any guns when we go to Churchill's house. There's no reason for gunplay just because Jim Dancer was seen riding out on open range.'

'Sheriff, Dancer climbed on Augustin for a reason!' Murfee snapped. 'Those men wanted to push trouble.'

Shepperd's voice tightened. 'If you come with me, you leave your sixguns holstered in my office. We got a good law here. We do it my way. That's the only way you'll go with me.'

Murfee's hand slapped the butt of his Colt. The sharp clap of his open palm against the solid bone handle was loud in the silence of the street.

Slattery said, 'We'll leave our guns in the jail, Steve.' His hard stare moved to Augustin, then shifted to Myron Blumberg and Teller. 'Then we'll go out and talk to Dancer.'

CHAPTER SIX

Ketchuck, the land agent, gripped the knob of Marshall Churchill's kitchen door. 'Those settlers will ask why I'm not in my office,' he said to Ralph Goodlove. 'Slattery and the other two were headed this way with Shepperd after they turned in their guns. I have to get back and open up so they won't know I came out to warn you.'

'You ran along the town's backside?' Goodlove asked. 'You stayed behind the houses? They didn't see you?'

The rancher's voice was held down, almost casual, and he kept the five men and woman in the room with him quiet and calm. He had been talking to Dancer, Jones, Torrey, and the Churchills when the land agent had pounded on the back door. Goodlove had stepped to the window and had kept his body behind the lace curtains while he looked out to see who knocked. Clara Churchill, a bony, work-worn, gray-haired woman, stood quietly behind her husband's chair as she had when Ketchuck told of the sheriff, Myron Blumberg, and the pot-and-pan drummer hurrying from the jail to meet the man named Slattery. Marshall Churchill, sitting with his wounded leg on a footstool, did not move.

Goodlove stared from the kitchen to the front door and waited for Shepperd to knock. 'Just stay calm,' he told the others. 'Nothing will happen.'

Ketchuck turned the doorknob. He watched Goodlove. 'If they see me here,' he said, 'they'll figure out everything. I should have been in my office waiting to meet those people.'

Dancer motioned toward the front door. 'We could take them right here.' He nodded at the Churchills and Ketchuck. 'We got witnesses to say Shepperd was the one who started shootin'.' He backed past the sink with its long-handled pump and opened the door to the broom closet. Three gunbelts with their holstered weapons hung from nails that jutted out as clothes hooks. Dancer reached in to take down his set of pearl-handled .44 Colts. 'I say we—'

'Shut that door,' Goodlove said quietly. 'Leave the guns where they are.'

Dancer closed the closet door. Jones said, 'But we c'n get them before they come in off the porch. You know we gotta get rid of Shepperd and Slattery.' Ketchuck shook his head as if trying to drive away an annoying fly. 'Ralph, I'm going. I was fortunate nobody saw me. If you have a shootout, people will see me leaving. The whole plan will fail. All our planning will be wasted.'

Goodlove did not look around. 'There's not going to be any shootout,' he said. 'You saw Shepperd make them leave their guns inside his office.' He chuckled. 'That law-abiding fool. That damn fool.' Footsteps could be heard on the porch, then knocking rattled the front door. Goodlove glanced at Ketchuck. 'All right. Leave now. Stay behind the house when Clara lets them in. You'll get back to your office without being seen.'

Ketchuck opened the door and closed it softly behind him. Clara Churchill gripped the top of her husband's chair. 'One of you men help me move him into the bedroom. Please.'

'No,' Goodlove told her. 'Marsh stays right here. He's always in this kitchen when one of your neighbors comes in to visit with him. We're only visiting him, just like them. That's all we're doing here.'

'Mr. Goodlove,' the woman said, 'this Slattery is looking for his two men. When they're found, he could tie Marsh's wound to what happened.'

'A broken leg? Shepperd would have told Slattery about that already. Don't act as though there is any reason to worry. Let them in.'

The knocks sounded again while Clara Churchill moved through the small hallway. She hesitated a moment, smoothed out the front of her dress, then opened the door.

Ben Shepperd stood directly in front of the doorway, his stubby body blocking the woman from having a full view of the five men behind him. 'Clara, we want to see Jim Dancer,' the lawman said. 'Is he here?'

'Yes, come in,' she answered. 'They're in the kitchen with Marshall.' She stepped back so the sheriff could move past her. She knew the tall man behind Shepperd was Slattery. Her glance flicked across the flat planes of his dark-burned face and his black hair parted deep on the right side. She closed the door after Myron Blumberg, Teller, a second cattlehand, and a Mexican had entered.

Watching the silent, serious men follow one another through the hall, she felt suddenly empty and lost inside. She shivered. It was not just because these men had crowded into her home, but because of the look on one man's face, the hard coldness she saw in Slattery's eyes.

Ben Shepperd nodded to Churchill. 'Sorry we have to come in like this, Marsh,' he said. He turned to Teller and pointed his finger at Dancer. 'That the man you saw near those two riders? Five days ago?'

'His horse, I saw,' the drummer answered.

'What is this?' Dancer asked angrily. 'What two riders?'

Ralph Goodlove said, 'Hold it, Jim. What is this all about, Ben?'

Shepperd watched Dancer. 'Mr. Teller saw the two men Slattery's lookin' for. They were camped out on the Big Horn six days ago. He saw Dancer out that way the next mornin'.'

'What?' said Dancer. 'He didn't see me out of this valley in a month. I ain't left Mr. Goodlove's ranch during that time 'cept to handle cattle. And to fight grass fires.'

'That's right. He ain't been away from the ranch,' Calem Torrey agreed. 'None of us have.' The redhead eyed Dancer and Goodlove. 'Mr. Goodlove, we been workin' twenty hours a day since the drought set in. You ain't lettin' anyone push Dancer into anythin'.'

Steve Murfee said, 'Sheriff, you've got a witness who'll swear that man was seen near where Huffaker and McDonald camped. I don't know why we're wastin' time.'

'Dancer wasn't out of the valley. None of us were,' the redheaded cowhand repeated. 'Mr. Goodlove, I don't like to see Dancer railroaded. I damn well don't.'

'That's enough, Calem,' Goodlove said. The cowhand seemed about to answer the rancher, and Goodlove's voice tightened. 'Enough, I told you.' He added, quieter, to Shepperd, 'Ben, Teller says he saw Dancer five days ago. That would be last Friday.' He looked at Churchill. 'Marsh broke his leg on Friday fighting that grass fire up in my north section. You saw us bring him in. You saw Jim Dancer was with us, if you'll remember.' He turned to Blumberg. 'We bought bandage and plaster for a cast from you. You saw my men bring Marsh in. He was in the light wagon, and Dancer was driving. You think back, Myron.'

Blumberg's face was deeply lined. Slowly, he nodded. His eyes met Slattery's. 'It's true. I saw the wagon drive past my store. Dancer was in the driver's seat. I'm sorry. We were wrong about this.'

Slattery said, 'What time did they bring him in?'

Blumberg thought for a moment. 'Afternoon. Early. One o'clock. Between one and one-thirty, I'd say.'

54

'Then they had time to get back to their ranch.' Slattery looked at Shepperd.

The lawman's eyes showed doubt and he said, 'Teller saw your two men the day before, he saw Dancer.' He began to shake his head.

'How about those three jumpin' Augustin?' Murfee said. 'They were lookin' for trouble. That could tie in.'

Goodlove said, 'Sheriff, if you want to hold Dancer, you arrest him. I'll appear in court for him. Every man with him in this room will appear too. And Mrs. Churchill. That trouble in the street had nothing to do with the men Slattery sent ahead. It was a mistake.'

'Only because we didn't get a chance to finish what we started,' Torrey said. 'We ain't hidin' the fact we don't cotton to all them Texans comin' in and takin' over the valley.'

Goodlove turned on the cowhand. 'That's enough,' he snapped. 'You work for me, you hold down that kind of talk.' He watched Slattery, then nodded to Shepperd. 'I've already told you. I regret that incident, Ben. It won't happen again. You decide. You take Dancer, I'll put up bail.'

'Well, I don't know,' the lawman began. He studied Teller. 'You didn't see Dancer, just his horse.'

'Yes. Just his horse.' The drummer was flustered now, not as sure of himself. 'I never said I saw Dancer close up. I didn't.'

Goodlove said, 'Mr. Slattery, do you want to

55

prefer charges?'

Murfee answered, 'Your men want trouble, Goodlove. I don't know why they do, but you control them. It's clear to me you do.'

The sheriff cut off his words. 'Won't be no charges, Ralph.' He nodded to Churchill and to Churchill's wife. 'Marsh, if there's anythin' I c'n do, you just call.' Shepperd swung around and waited for Augustin to lead the way through the front hall.

Clara Churchill followed the lawman, Slattery, and the others to the door. As soon as the woman clicked the latch closed behind them, Calem Torrey cursed.

'Now's the time to take care of them bastards!' he snarled. He stepped to the broom closet and reached out his right hand to open the door.

Goodlove grabbed hold of the redheaded cowhand's arm and stopped him. 'When they aren't armed?' he questioned. 'You damned fool! I wouldn't get hold of a Longhorn steer before a federal lawman was sent into this valley!' He scanned the watching faces, pausing until he had himself completely under control. 'Don't leave until I get back. I know what to do to get ownership of that cattle legally.'

'What about Teller?' Dancer asked. 'He could remember the direction them two headed when they broke camp. That damn drummer's got to be shut up.'

'You'll do nothing about him. None of you will do or say anything until I tell you to.' Goodlove's features softened as he stared down at Churchill. 'You were fine while they were in here, Marsh. Both you and Clara. Just stick it out. I'll make it worth your while.' All trace of tenderness vanished when he again faced his other three men. 'Don't leave this house until I get back.' He opened the door and went outside.

Goodlove walked fast to catch up with Shepperd and Slattery before they reached the jail. The six men were grouped close together. Ben Shepperd did most of the talking, his attention on Teller. Beyond the intersection at Four Corners, seven white-topped carretas and ranch wagons were drawn up at the hitchrails. Most of the women and children who moved about the porches and walks or went into Blumberg's store were strangers to Goodlove. Their husbands and fathers had been let into the government land building by Ketchuck. If there was any complaint about having been made to wait, Goodlove could not tell from the calm, orderly way the men acted.

One of the women on the general store porch started down the steps when Slattery reached the building. She was wearing a blue dress, her long dark hair tied neatly along the nape of her neck. She was a fine looking woman, beautiful even, with a figure that made him want to keep watching her. But while he approached the sheriff and Slattery, Goodlove gave his attention only to the two men.

Shepperd was telling the fat pot-and-pan salesman he could leave Yellowstone City. Teller nodded. He looked toward Goodlove as the rancher stepped into the group and stopped alongside Slattery.

'Mr. Slattery,' Goodlove said, 'I didn't get a chance to discuss the price of cattle with you. I'd like to have papers drawn up.'

Slattery turned to the rancher, aware of the silence which suddenly fell around them. 'Our price was twenty-five dollars in Dodge,' he said bluntly. 'It's thirty here.'

Goodlove shook his head. 'I told you about the drought. I can't pay more than twenty. You won't get more than that from the other ranchers. I'm paying top price.'

Two men who had left the land office stepped off the walk to join at the rear of the gathering. One settler made a low remark to the other, both showing dissatisfaction at the figure Goodlove stated. They looked at Slattery and he clearly spoke up for them. 'It's not enough,' he said. 'Our people need more cash on hand for land and homes.'

Again Goodlove shook his head. 'I wish I could offer more.' He watched the faces, aware that the dissatisfaction had deepened into antagonism. He shrugged his shoulders, looking apologetically at the men and the women who had come down from the porches to listen. His eyes met Judy Fiske's for an instant, and he added, 'Possibly, after all of you get settled, we can talk. I'm the main rancher in the valley. I'd like to have my cowhands move the cattle I buy onto my land now. But I've stated the best price I can, so I'll just have to wait.'

'You'll wait a good long time,' Steve Murfee said. 'As long as there's a bank we can borrow from.' The men and women nodded their heads. A few made remarks of agreement that grew into conversation.

'That's it,' Slattery said. 'We'll sell, but you and anyone else who wants to buy has to meet our price.' Each man present echoed his statement.

Goodlove nodded. Slattery would remember he had quoted his price in the open, the men and women would remember, Shepperd would remember. 'I don't believe anyone will be able to beat my offer,' he said. 'Not the way things have been in this territory.'

He turned away, letting his gaze slide across Judy Fiske's face before he began to retrace his steps toward the residential section.

The Texans would get their bank loans, he knew, because the government had set up The Homestead Act in such a way that no one could stop the purchase of land. But Goodlove had made plans for something like this happening, and Ketchuck in the land office was his man. The Customary Range Act would be argued in the United States Congress before the end of the present session. The passage of that law, time, the summer and fall droughts, and the hard winter which would last five or six long months, would give him what he wanted in Calligan Valley. Dancer, Jones, and Torrey had laid the groundwork for trouble. It would come. And he would have every foot of land and every head of Longhorn cattle he wanted.

Goodlove turned into Churchill's yard and walked briskly up the steps onto the new front porch. Teller, and what the drummer had seen, did not bother him. Or Ben Shepperd, with his straight-line following the exact letter of the law . . .

Slattery was the one man who could stand in his way. The fine-looking woman who had left Blumberg's store to meet Slattery appeared to be Slattery's woman. Goodlove thoughtfully rubbed the thumb of his right hand along the round of his jawbone before he gripped the doorknob. Everything had a price. He had only to learn the price and be willing to pay it. It would be like paying for the wood and labor which went into building Churchill's porch. Seeing Slattery's woman, knowing she could be the kind who could match a man like himself, wanting her, gave him another reason for getting rid of Slattery.

That was exactly what he meant to do . . .

CHAPTER SEVEN

Slattery and Judy Fiske bent over the land office counter and studied the large inked diagram of Calligan Valley which Ketchuck had drawn for prospective settlers. Every available foot of graze land was shown. It was good land, most of it, yet Slattery could not tell exactly how much area Goodlove's Circle G Ranch covered. If Goodlove was able to buy all the cattle he wanted, he had to own more than just the ten acres prescribed by The Homestead Act. Even a hundred acres would not keep a large herd alive, especially during the Montana winters. He wondered more about Goodlove and the power and influence the rancher had in the Territory. He said nothing about this to Judy. She was too happy planning the acreage she would buy, wanting it to be next to his ten acres so she could make more plans.

'Then we'll take these two sections,' Judy said to him. 'Side by side.' She smiled widely at him and pressed her shoulder against his. 'Then when we're married, we'll have all this land.' She traced her finger along the bend of the river. 'We'll never have to want for grass or water. Or enough room for our children.'

He grinned and said, 'You're moving a little too fast for me.' His face became serious again. 'We'll sign the list for each section, but I want to look them over first. Winter hits early and stays long.'

Judy smiled. 'Mm-mn. It does.'

Slattery liked the feeling of having her close. He had been so busy since leaving Texas, so on-the-go day after day, night after night during the drive, that he had been able to spend only a few hours alone with her. He hadn't held her in such a long time, the two of them talking, planning. Ian Huffaker and Fred McDonald were on his mind constantly now, along with the trouble with Goodlove's men. He had neither the time nor the mind to spend the day planning. He glanced across his shoulder and out through the window. The town square was practically empty. Two of the white-topped wagons were still tied to the hitchrails of the land office. Across the roadway, Teller's wagon waited at the general store rail alongside Mal Weaver's carreta. The sun's heat was abating and the buildings' shadows were lengthening, crawling from the west-side false fronts toward the wagons. Dusk would come soon, and Slattery wanted every family headed back to the camping grounds before dark.

'We'll ride out along the river flat first thing in the morning,' he told Judy. 'We'll have the whole day to look over every inch of the land you want.'

Judy glanced at the others studying the

diagram. Steve Murfee and Lottie Wells were bent over with their heads close together, and Ed Anderson and his wife, and the Cullens were picking out their sites. 'Alone?' she said.

'Alone,' he repeated. Grinning, he printed the names 'Fiske' and 'Slattery' across the two open sections. He nodded to Ketchuck, then he and Judy stepped outside onto the porch, not speaking but each knowing what the other thought.

The hazy summer dusk seemed to rise from the valley floor as the sun dropped behind the southwestern peaks. A soft grayness settled over the town and river. Already tiny sparks of fireflies glowed on and off among the willows, cottonwoods, and alders. In the first half hour before full darkness, Yellowstone City showed only quiet and peace, giving a stark irony to the threat and promise of violence Slattery had felt in Churchill's home. Beside him Judy touched his arm. 'It's just what we wanted,' she said. 'It's worth the hard work and waiting.'

'It will be,' he answered. He took her hand to cross toward Blumberg's store.

Cal Teller's wagon, part home for the drummer and part storage space for his wares, showed years of use and travel. Teller's tired-looking roan horse waited patiently while the salesman arranged his boxes in the rear. The sign, KITCHEN UTENSILS, painted on the wooden side was faded and spotted from the sun and dust. Teller looked up from his work when Judy and Slattery reached him. He dropped the last box onto the tailgate and said, 'I'm leaving now. I want to get clear of the foothills by midnight.'

Slattery said, 'Thanks for going into that house with us. We appreciate your trying.'

Teller nodded. 'That, yes . . . yes,' he answered quickly. 'I did what I could. I'm sorry I couldn't help more.'

'We'll be needing some of your pans,' Slattery told him. 'On your next trip in.'

The drummer nodded again, too quickly. He glanced around at the porch. Myron Blumberg watched through the store's long front window. 'Myron will have anything you need, Mr. Slattery. If he doesn't, he'll send me a letter.' He walked around to the wagon's step plate and climbed up into the seat.

Judy and Slattery paused while the drummer turned the wagon and headed westward. Myron Blumberg met them inside his store. The elderly storekeeper's thin face was deeply lined. 'Cal's afraid,' he said, watching Teller drive toward the brush and trees which screened the log bridge. 'I offered to let him use one of my rooms, but he's afraid of Goodlove's men. I could have asked Ben Shepperd to make him stay.'

'Let him go,' Slattery said. 'He did what he could.' He glanced to the left, past the boot and shoe counter. Mal Weaver walked toward them carrying a box of supplies. His wife and

64

daughter had halted momentarily at the toy counter. Weaver looked around and called for them to hurry.

'You headin' out now, Mal?' Slattery asked.

'Yes, if these two females of mine ever make up their minds.'

'That drummer will be just ahead of you,' Slattery told him. 'Have Lute Canby follow him as far as the foothills. Jim Magoun can go with Canby. Make sure Teller's all right.'

Weaver nodded briskly. 'Nan,' he said across his shoulder, 'you and Linda come along now.'

Weaver's light-haired wife continued to hesitate near the toys. Her daughter, a six-year-old who resembled her mother, hugged a rag doll in both of her arms and watched her father. 'She wants the doll,' Nancy Weaver explained. 'I told her we can't afford it.'

'She can take it,' Myron Blumberg said. 'Today's special. A toy for every boy or girl who comes in with their Mama or Papa.' The small man smiled at the child who hugged the doll tighter and beamed up at the storekeeper. 'Tell the other children.'

The little girl's 'Thank you' was lost under her father's loud laugh when he said, 'There's twenty-two kids with us, Mr. Blumberg. Twenty-three when Ruth Koski delivers.'

'Twenty-three presents.' The storekeeper ruffled the girl's blonde curls as she went past him. Mal Weaver's laugh quieted and he said to Slattery, 'I had the land agent hold the section next to us for the Huffakers. We'll be goin' out to look at it in the mornin'.'

'Good,' Slattery said 'We'll be riding out too.' He moved up the aisle when Judy tugged on his sleeve, and he laughed as Mal Weaver said behind him, 'Oh, man. Bein' led around like that and you're not even hitched yet.'

*   *   *

Ralph Goodlove stood at the side window of the Churchills' living room. He had been standing in the same spot staring past the lace curtains since Dancer called into the kitchen to tell him Teller's wagon was leaving Yellowstone City. The palms of Goodlove's hands were wet, and he wiped the perspiration on his pants leg. He did not like what he had to do. He did not like being forced by the actions of other men. But Slattery had seen to it that Ben Shepperd came to this house to question one of his men, and the loud-mouthed drummer had to be shut up. Teller might remember more of what he had seen.

Dancer, standing at one of the room's two front windows, said, 'Another wagon's leavin' town, Boss. Just goin' out.'

Goodlove watched the low-slung carreta, its canvas top gray in the rising darkness. It rolled fast, too, as though the driver was trying to catch up with the first wagon. That was possible, if Slattery or Shepperd thought there would be any danger to the drummer once he was clear of the town.

'I can get out with Calem,' Dancer offered, 'make damn sure nothin' goes wrong.'

'No. Slattery is still in town,' Goodlove said. 'I want him to see you here when he leaves. We won't give him the slightest reason to connect you to the drummer.'

Dancer let the curtain fall back into place. He rubbed both of his hands along his hips and shifted his stance, bending forward slightly with the readiness of a gunfighter. 'I have reason to call Slattery. What was said about me goes further than just that drummer.'

Goodlove stepped away from the window. He shook his head. 'Torrey will take care of Teller. He'll handle whoever is driving that carreta if he has to.' He turned to face Marsh Churchill, lying on the cowhide sofa, and his wife who kneeled on the carpetless floor while she changed the bandage on her husband's wounded leg. Churchill's jaws were bitten tight, his eyes closed. Goodlove said to Clam Churchill, 'When they come we should be eating.'

The woman's bony face was drawn from worry. 'Isn't there a way you can call in a doctor! His leg is so swollen and I don't know how to stop the infection.'

'It's draining,' Goodlove said. 'It will clear up.'

'But it's so hot and painful. Mr. Goodlove, we only have three weeks, a month at the longest, before the snow starts. The pass could be blocked with snow.'

Goodlove shook his head and studied Churchill, knowing the man was suffering. 'You'll have to hold on, Marsh. A doctor would see that's a bullet wound and know you didn't break your leg falling from your horse. All we need is for Slattery to learn you were shot. Sooner or later somebody will find those two Texans and they'll see they both have bullets in them.'

Churchill's eyes shifted to his wife. 'Get supper,' he said softly.

'Marsh,' she pleaded, 'the infection could spread through you. Once the snow hits, we won't be able to get a doctor. A doctor won't travel all the distance from Bozeman.'

'Do what Mr. Goodlove says,' her husband told her, his voice rising. 'He'll take care of us.'

Clara Churchill straightened and stared fearfully at Goodlove. 'After this Slattery is dead, you will move my husband.' Her tone changed, became demanding, on the point of being hysterical. 'If the infection doesn't clear up, you will move him!'

Goodlove stepped around the sofa closer to the woman. He kept his voice quiet and calm to reassure her. 'I will,' he promised. 'The minute Slattery is out of the way, I'll personally take Marsh out of the valley to a

68

doctor. Don't you worry. Marsh was the one who stopped those two. I don't forget.'

Clara looked down at her husband and nodded. 'You do owe him.' Her stare rose and moved from Goodlove to Dancer. 'You all owe Marsh,' she added, 'and you'll keep your word.' She walked from the sofa past Goodlove and Dancer and went through the living room doorway into the kitchen.

CHAPTER EIGHT

Mal Weaver sat contentedly on the wagon seat, the leather reins held lightly between his fingers. Linda talked and babied her doll in the rear of the carreta. Nancy sat beside him and said very little. It was one of his wife's ways, he knew, when she was content and happy. There was reason to be. The section of land he had the agent hold for him was exactly what they had wanted. They had enough acreage for the cattle he'd keep and there was also room toward the south for Linda to build her own home when she grew up and married. He found it strange to be thinking of that now, with the child so young. But Mal had hope, a hope he hadn't felt before. The bank loan would be approved. He thought of how the manager of Yellowstone City's bank had filled out the papers for the loan, and of the ten acres of land he would soon own. His thoughts were on his wife and daughter, riding safe so close to him, when he heard the whinny of a horse come from the trees ahead. The sounds were loud in the rising dusk, and Mal reached under the wagon seat for his Springfield rifle.

The clustered willows, cottonwoods, and alders blotted a clear view of the river, though he could see where the log bridge began. Fireflies flickered and glowed along the water's surface and up into the brush. As the wagon rolled closer to the bridge, mosquitoes descended on them in great humming clouds.

'Look! Isn't that the drummer's wagon!' Nancy suddenly said.

Weaver saw the drummer's wagon. The vehicle had somehow gone off the far side of the bridge, landing on its side in the deepest part of the river. The driver's seat was completely under water and there was no sign of the drummer. His horse had fought to save itself from drowning, but hitched firmly to the wagon, the battle had been hopeless.

Weaver whipped his mules to make them move faster. He laid the rifle on the seat and prepared to jump down as soon as he reached the end of the bridge. Then, quickly, he again grabbed the weapon.

'You!' he called. 'Stop! Stop right there!'

The man he saw climbing onto the far bank had been hidden by the overhanging brush, yet it was clear he was trying to reach the horse

Weaver had heard snort and whinny beyond the trees. The man crouched low and ran once he was on the bank. Weaver aimed the Springfield and fired.

'Daddy! Daddy!' he heard Linda cry. Nancy was climbing over the seat to hold the child and keep her out of the line of fire.

'Stay down!' Weaver yelled. 'Both of you lie flat!' He triggered off a second shot, expecting the fleeing man to return his fire. The man did not slow his run. Bent low, hugging the ground, he vanished into the timber and darkness. Weaver fired once more and sent another bullet through the woods where he judged the man had left his horse. Then he drew in on the reins to stop his mules.

He knew before he climbed off the wagon that Cal Teller was dead. He could see the drummer's body pinned under the seat, barely visible in the water's blackness. Weaver did not know whether or not the man who had run had jumped the pot-and-pan salesman from a tree or if he had been waiting on the bridge. But he had staked out his horse and waited out here to kill Teller.

Weaver heard his daughter whimper. He looked around at his wagon, not wanting the little girl or his wife to see the dead man. 'Stay down,' he told them. 'Nan, keep Linda down. Just calm her.' He aimed the Springfield rifle into the air. His gunfire had been heard and someone would be coming from town. He

71

knew Tom Slattery would come out. He fired twice, once in anger because a man had been so brutally murdered, and again to make certain Tom and the other men would hurry and help him.

*   *   *

Slattery kicked his horse's flank and the black gelding ran harder. The initial cracks of a rifle had been distant, snapping noises inside the general store. But when Slattery had run onto the porch, the final two shots came as sharp bangs that blasted from the streambed and echoed through the town and into the foothills. Ben Shepperd had appeared from the jail, Steve Murfee dashed out of the land office. Now, both men rode behind Slattery, kicking and spurring their mounts to catch up with the black gelding before Slattery reached the river.

There was no moon. Only the stars overhead, which multiplied in number as the sky grew darker and darker, gave light enough for Slattery to see Weaver's carreta stopped on the log bridge. Weaver had gone off the high south bank and was looking at Cal Teller's wagon in the water. While he reined in his horse, Slattery could hear Linda Weaver crying inside the carreta. Her mother spoke softly, trying to calm her.

Weaver looked across his shoulder as

Slattery hurried down to him. The sound of horses' hoofbeats drummed on the flat to the west. Three or four horses and riders headed into town from beyond the trees. The clomping of Murfee's big buckskin and the sheriff's roan rumbled on the log bridge. 'That drummer's pinned under his wagon,' Weaver told Slattery. 'He was jumped and driven off the bridge, and I saw the one who did it. I got off three shots at him.'

'Did you hit him?' asked Slattery.

'Don't think so.' Weaver glanced around at his carreta. His daughter's crying had calmed. Weaver's voice was very quiet. 'We could've been shot if we'd been close enough. Whoever killed the drummer made sure he was dead. He went into the water to be certain.'

Murfee and Shepperd swung off their horses and came to the edge of the bank. The sheriff heard Weaver's last few words. He stared down at the overturned wagon. The water was black dark, yet the hazy starshine made it possible to see the white of Teller's shirt below the surface.

'There was no chance to pull him out?' Shepperd said.

'He was in the river before I reached the bridge. The man I shot at must have been makin' sure he was dead when he heard my wagon comin'.'

'Did you get a good look at him?'

'It was too dark. But I think . . .' Weaver

73

stopped talking and turned to the bridge the instant his wife called from the carreta. 'Mal,' she said, 'you didn't see him clear enough. You couldn't have.'

'Mother, you take care of the child,' Weaver told her. He motioned toward the brush and timber along the banking. 'He wasn't too tall, and I think he had red hair.'

Slattery looked at Shepperd. 'That enough for you, Sheriff?'

Shepperd did not answer. The three horses that approached from the southwest came past the trees and onto the bridge. Lute Canby, the lead rider, called out, 'Mal, Tom, is everything all right? Any you people hurt?'

'We're all right,' Steve Murfee answered. Canby, Ray Bishop, and Ted Johnson, each man a husband, father, or member of one of the families that had taken part in the trail drive, stopped their mounts and stared down at the overturned wagon.

Bishop swung out of the saddle. 'How'd a horse and wagon roll off like that?' he asked.

Weaver started to tell them what he had seen. Slattery stepped closer to Ben Shepperd. 'Sheriff, you know why this was done. Either we take in Torrey as your deputies or we'll go after him on our own. That drummer saw our two men and he saw Dancer. Torrey's job was to shut him up. He's not getting away with it.'

Shepperd nodded. 'The badges are in my office,' he said. He took his bridle and led his

74

horse away from the carreta before he mounted. Slattery and Murfee followed him with their horses. Mal Weaver said to Bishop, 'Take Nancy and the baby back to camp. I'll borrow your horse.'

'Sure, Mal.'

Nancy Weaver leaned over in the wagon seat. 'Don't go, Mal,' she said. 'I don't care if we have to go back to Texas. I don't want trouble.'

'If we can prove I did see Torrey, we can tie Dancer to Ian and Fred McDonald,' her husband told her. 'I'm goin' in.' Holding his Springfield rifle in his left hand, he gripped the horn of Bishop's saddle to climb onto the horse.

*   *   *

Slattery and Murfee rode from the bridge with Ben Shepperd. Lamps had been lighted in almost all of the buildings along the main street. Streams of light from windows and doors splashed in broad yellow squares across porches and walks. The people who had come out of the stores, saloon, and their homes when they heard the gunfire had gathered at the intersection of Four Corners. The sheriff, Murfee, and Slattery rode in silence until Mal Weaver joined them. Slattery began to angle his black gelding toward the residential section, but the sheriff stayed in the middle of the street.

'Torrey won't be at Churchill's house once he hears we've been sworn in,' Slattery said. 'We'd do better to take him before he has a chance to get away.'

'You don't carry guns without wearin' a badge,' the lawman answered. 'This will go to court. I'm not deputizing Weaver. I want him as a witness.' He pointed ahead, nodding to Slattery. 'That Mexican is one of your men. The no-gun law is for him same as anyone else.'

Augustin Vierra had stepped off the general store porch into the center of the roadway. He waited well clear of the town citizens. He carried a Winchester carbine and watched the sheriff, Slattery, and the others as though he expected there would be trouble.

'Nothing happened to the Weavers, Augustin,' Slattery called. The Mexican did not shift his stance. He simply waited. Judy Fiske and Lottie Wells stood side by side near Myron Blumberg in the doorway of his store. The land agent, Ketchuck, and Philip Lashway, the bank president, waited in the doorways of their buildings. Closer to Vierra now, Slattery said, 'Get inside with your carbine, Augustin. Stay with Judy and Lottie. Keep them inside.'

The Mexican nodded. Murfee said, 'Watch it, Tom. There's Goodlove.' The rancher had appeared from the direction of Churchill's

76

home. Dancer and Waco Jones were with him. None of the three men either held or wore a weapon.

Ben Shepperd kneed his horse out ahead of Slattery's gelding and Murfee's buckskin. 'I'll handle this,' the lawman told them.

Murfee's glance moved from building to building, the porches, doorways, windows, and the false fronts. His hand rested on the stock of the Winchester booted beneath his right knee. Slattery touched the cattlehand's arm. 'Do what he says, Steve.'

Murfee raised his hand, but he kept it close to his knee. Vierra stayed at his left, watching to see what would happen. Ben Shepperd stopped his horse in front of Goodlove. 'Calem Torrey killed the drummer who just left town,' the sheriff told the rancher. 'I'm goin' after him.'

Goodlove glanced at Dancer and Jones, then returned his attention to the lawman. 'Are you certain, Ben? Calem left for my ranch more than half an hour ago. He rode north, not southwest.'

Mal Weaver edged his mount in between Slattery and Shepperd. 'I saw the man who killed Teller. He was short and redheaded. I might've wounded him.'

Dancer swore obscenely. He started to make a remark, but Goodlove spoke first looking straight at the sheriff. His stare shifted for a moment, sliding across the faces of the townspeople who had moved closer to hear what was being said. 'I'm one of those who were looking forward to the Texans settling in the valley, Ben. But there's been so much trouble. First Dancer is accused of killing two men.'

'Killing?' Slattery questioned. 'No one said those men were dead.'

Goodlove's eyes snapped to Slattery. 'That was what you meant in Churchill's house.' His tone was rising, showing anger for the first time. He continued, his words louder, directed more to the onlookers than the men he faced. 'I had my cowhands ride into town today without wearing their guns. You people know that. You know it, Ben.' He gestured at Dancer and Jones. 'They will be armed from now on, for their own protection.' He paused, judging the quiet talk that began among the townspeople. 'I know I can't stop you from buying land in our valley, Slattery. The government has opened this territory for settlement. But I don't like the trouble you've brought with you. There's no reason for it, and I'd just as soon have everyone in this town know I don't like it.'

Slattery was as aware as Goodlove of the controlled but angry grumble among the people. He said, 'Weaver had a good look at the man who ran from the drummer's wagon. His description fits Calem Torrey. The sheriff is swearing in deputies to go after him. If you're so much for having law and order in the valley, you'll show who you back.'

The mutter and mumble again swept through the crowd. All talk died to an expectant silence as Goodlove snapped his answer.

'If one of my men does anything wrong, I'll go after him as soon as any one of you.' He glanced around at the faces, asking for understanding. 'I want Calem to have a chance to tell his side. I'll ride out with Sheriff Shepperd. I'll do what I can to help handle—'

'The law'll handle him, Mr. Goodlove,' Shepperd interrupted. 'You ride with me, you take orders like everyone else.'

Goodlove shook his head. 'Not as part of a lynching party. I'll wear your badge. If Calem's guilty, the law will have him. I promise. But I mean to see he has his chance to have his say.' Once more he scanned the faces, seeing the men and women nodding to his words. He turned on his heels and pushed past the listeners between himself and the jail.

Ben Shepperd swung his horse and watched the rancher, trailed by Dancer and Waco Jones, cross the boardwalk and go into the jail office. The sheriff had not missed the hasty, respectful movements of the people who had rushed to back away and open a path for the three. Slattery also knew what the townspeople's reaction meant. He pulled King around slowly, careful not to bump or brush

79

one of the men or women. Not one of the people spoke to him, Murfee, or Augustin Vierra. Their stares were openly unfriendly, distrustful. It was what Goodlove had wanted. They and the other Texans who had made the trail drive had been in Calligan Valley less than eight hours, and an open hate had already been carefully, cleverly built up. The actions of the rancher's hired hands, each word Goodlove had spoken, everything he had done, had been to turn the people against them.

Slattery slowed King alongside Augustin Vierra. 'You start Judy and Lottie and the last two wagons back to camp,' he told the Mexican .'Mal and Nancy will be with you.'

'Si,' Vierra said. While Slattery continued on with Shepperd, Augustin walked over to Judy Fiske and Lottie Wells who waited on the general store porch.

* * *

Stepping across the boardwalk to go into the sheriff's office, Ralph Goodlove was in complete control of himself. He had succeeded out in the street, he knew. Control was as important now as it had been in front of the townspeople. Shepperd's opinion and Slattery's realization that everything had been planned did not matter. The town would be here after Slattery, the sheriff, and everyone else who tried to stop him had been taken care of. Goodlove had known he would have to face an open fight sooner or later, and its coming now did not bother him. He had planned for that, calmly, always in control of himself and the situation, as he was in control now.

The sheriff's office was a small room with white-washed walls and a small cell block of two iron-barred cubicles beyond the gunrack. Goodlove stopped near two cane-backed chairs along one wall. He did not turn, simply spoke softly to Dancer. 'Go get Torrey,' he said. 'He's hiding in Churchill's barn. Tell him we'll be riding out to the ranch with Shepperd. I want Slattery shot when he's crossing the bridge.'

'Torrey mighta kept runnin', Mr. Goodlove. I'll go out ahead into the river brush—'

'Get Torrey. He was told to circle back to Churchill's after he took care of that drummer. I want him waiting when we start out.'

'But someone might see him leavin' town and tell Shepperd. No one's watchin' for me.'

Goodlove turned and looked out through the open doorway, standing as though he waited patiently while Shepperd, Slattery, and Murfee dismounted at the hitchrails beyond the office window.

'Leave before Shepperd swears me in,' he said. 'Tell Calem it will be dark enough and I'll see to it there's enough confusion for him to get away. He'll have only one shot at Slattery.

He has to be sure he makes it good.'

CHAPTER NINE

Crouching low so he wouldn't be seen, Calem
Torrey ran from the brush one-hundred yards
east of Churchill's house to the rear door
of Churchill's barn. Streams of yellowish
lamplight beamed down from the kitchen and
bedroom windows, and lamps were on in the
homes on each side of Churchill's. Nobody was
outside searching the yards. Torrey's respect
for Goodlove deepened. Goodlove had based
his plans on exactly what he believed Shepperd
would do once the pot-and-pan drummer was
found. Never would the lawman think the one
who killed the big-mouthed salesman would
double back into town and hide.

Torrey opened the barn door, stepped
inside, and slid the iron bolt into place. There
was no yelling or shouting from Four Corners.
Goodlove was right about the people too. He
had depended on their not really caring as
long as the death of the drummer didn't effect
them or their families. He was glad he'd tied in
with Goodlove and that now the rancher owed
him. He had done as Goodlove planned, riding
hard and fast north along the flat, until he
knew for certain he wasn't trailed. Then he
circled back to Yellowstone City, striking the

river east of town and staying in the timber and brush until he reached a spot behind Churchill's.

His horse was well hidden in a thicket and ground-tied with enough rope to reach water and grass so it would have no reason to whinny or snort or make other sounds which would lead someone to him. That was the one thing that had gone wrong, damn it, the horse being heard by that stupid bastard of a Texas dirt-eater who'd made the trail drive. And he'd just barely missed being shot climbing the river bank and getting away.

Torrey walked through the barn to the high double front doors, smelling the good smells of hay and leather and horseflesh, and being careful not to spook Churchill's stallion or his team mare. He set the heavy carbine down barrel-up against a framing four-by-four and carefully, silently, pushed the door open so he could see. Beyond the trees where the log bridge crossed the stream, torches flickered, lighting the blackness of the water.

They were pulling the drummer out. Damn his luck. Another half-minute and he would have been clear of the wagon. He'd had to go down into the water to be positive Teller had drowned and that it looked like the drummer had gone over himself. The smash he'd given Teller on the head after dropping into his wagon from a tree would seem to have happened when the horse and wagon went off the bridge . . .

Torrey caught his breath and closed the door. He'd heard a sound from near the house. The crunch of a footfall on the sand. Someone was walking toward the barn.

He grabbed the carbine and brought it up as he would a sixgun. The scuff of boots approached. Torrey backed away from the door. He tightened his finger on the trigger, waiting for the door to be opened. The starshine would give him a clear target.

'Calem? Calem?' he heard Jim Dancer's voice say through the door. 'Calem, you in there?'

'Dancer,' Torrey whispered. 'Come 'round back.'

Dancer moved down alongside the barn while Torrey went to the rear door. Churchill's team horse nickered and rubbed its rump against the stallboards. No other sound came from inside or outside. Torrey quietly unhooked and opened the door, relatching it the instant Dancer stepped through. He turned to Dancer in the darkness, expecting to be told he had done a good job and that Goodlove was completely satisfied.

Dancer spoke in a whisper. 'They're lookin' for you. That sodbuster thinks he can identify you.' Torrey began to interrupt. Dancer went on faster, telling of the deputies being sworn in, and Goodlove's orders, then said, 'They'll be headed out of town for the ranch. You've got enough time to spot yourself near the bridge and get Slattery.'

Torrey shook his head. He was not able to read Dancer's face, yet he knew Jim Dancer would think the way he thought. 'There'll be five of them with Goodlove. I can't handle five.'

'Goodlove'll be behind them. I'm going out with Waco to get into the brush behind them. We'll finish all of them off at once. Don't worry, we'll cover you.'

Torrey did not wait another moment. He opened the door and went out into the dark and ran to the side of Churchill's house. The idea struck him then, while he pressed his spine against the front porch that Churchill had built with Goodlove's money. Why should he share in getting rid of Slattery with Dancer and Waco? If he took care of Slattery alone, Goodlove would owe him so much more than for shutting up the pot-and-pan drummer.

Torrey retraced his path to the rear of Churchill's house and started to run toward the general store alleyway, directly across from the jail. He was excited now, an excitement he knew must be held down. He'd been afraid Goodlove would blow up at his being seen in the river by the Texan, but here he was getting ready to settle everything for him.

Goodlove had Dancer, Waco Jones, and Chino Neill, who were all faster guns than he was. But now he was the one who would get rid of Slattery, and Shepperd too if he had the chance. The top lawman's job would be his for the asking once Goodlove owned the valley. Goodlove would own it. He would get ownership of every acre of land from the Texans, just like he'd eventually own every last head of the Longhorn cattle they had driven here. Goodlove had planned things too carefully. He would win in the end, and the men he valued and could trust would get the good jobs.

Torrey turned into the dark general store alleyway. He slowed, not wanting to be heard by anyone out in Four Corners.

He halted at the store porch, then stood with his spine pressed against the rough wooden boards as he had at Churchill's. He felt the cold chill of excitement while he edged his head around the corner of the porch to see across the street.

Five horses were tied at the rails near the sheriff's office. Shadows of men moved behind the office window. The entire square was brightly lit, the dirt road yellowish-white under the lamplight. Whenever the river breeze blew, small gritty halos whirled up around the porch lamps. Crouched in the dark, holding the carbine in both hands, Torrey waited. The last two wagons of Texans were moving slowly away from the store rails. A man and woman and their three children were in one wagon. The Mexican and two women, both good-

86

looking, had left Myron Blumberg and were in the other. None of them could give Slattery help. Shepperd and the men with Slattery would be too shocked to act fast enough once Slattery was hit . . .

The figures inside the jail walked toward the office door. Torrey grinned to himself and sprawled flat alongside the porch steps.

Ben Shepperd led the others outside, followed by the hardcase cattlehand with Slattery. Torrey aimed the carbine, the stock tight against his shoulder, his finger ready on the trigger. He squinted to see clearer through the lamplight. He didn't want to mistake Goodlove for Slattery. He had to make the first shot count. He could take no chance on missing.

*   *   *

'Watch the trees once we're near the bridge,' Ben Shepperd said. 'He used that spot before and could be waiting there again.'

'We're wastin' time,' Waco Jones, a step behind Murfee, said. 'You'll see Calem's out to Mr. Goodlove's ranch. You'll know he wasn't the one.'

The sheriff hesitated before he mounted. Goodlove crossed the walk after Jones, in front of Slattery. Shepperd looked directly at the rancher. 'You'll ride with me, Mr. Goodlove, so Torrey'll know we're not comin'' at him shootin'.'

'Mal will stay at the rear,' Slattery said, stepping from the office ahead of Weaver. 'Torrey or whoever did kill Teller must have seen him in his wagon.' He held his Winchester raised while his eyes flicked from the wagons that left town to the buildings along the street, the windows, porches, false fronts, and the dark mouths of the alleyways.

The sudden glint of lamplight on something was all he caught, but it was enough. He started to move to the right and backwards, shouting, 'The store alley! Watch it! Alongside the store porch!'

A weapon banged from the store alleyway. The bullet ripped through the brim of Slattery's hat in the same instant that Slattery triggered off a bullet, aiming low, knowing the bushwhacker lay prone behind the steps. He was pumping the carbine when a second shot banged from the alley and he was hit high on the right shoulder.

The sledgehammer impact of the bullet drove him back against the front of the jail. He tried to squeeze the trigger, but couldn't. He dropped to his knees, seeing the others, Goodlove and Jones included, fan out away from the horses, all firing toward the store alley. He felt no pain, yet it took his complete strength to stay conscious.

The bushwhacker fired again and again. Ben Shepperd was hit and fell like a heavy sack. Slattery kneeled on the boardwalk, holding his shoulder to stop the flow of blood. Murfee made a dash across the road. Weaver ran behind him. Slattery heard his name being called. 'Tom! Tom!'

Through his pain, past Shepperd's motionless body, he could see the wagons leaving town had stopped. Judy had jumped from the carreta seat and she shouted to him, 'Stay down! Don't try to stand!' as she ran toward him.

He wanted to yell and keep her away from him. He tried to push himself up, and the pain drove into him like a white-hot branding iron. His arms and hands had no strength. He fell forward onto his stomach, half conscious but aware of guns banging and of Judy Fiske, only a few feet from him, stumbling as though she had been thrown down headfirst by a great dark hazy hand that rushed at him and covered him completely while everything went black.

*   *   *

Running across the street, Murfee had fired five bullets at the bushwhacker. The gunman had left his cover, Murfee was sure, because no more shots came while he went up onto the porch and pressed himself against the storefront to listen before he went into the blackness of the alley. He couldn't hear a sound back there. Mal Weaver had disappeared into an alleyway further up the road, circling around behind the buildings to cut off any escape. Waco Jones had followed him.

Ralph Goodlove reached the porch and crowded in close to Murfee. 'Hear anything?' he questioned.

'Nothin'. I think he run.' He listened, aware that Ben Shepperd lay in the street and that Slattery was down on the boardwalk. Judy Fiske had fallen in the street and Lottie Wells had jumped from the wagon to help her. Shouting was heard from behind the barn. People had run out of their homes to learn what had happened.

Murfee jumped down into the thick darkness. He expected a shot from the rear of the alley, waited for it, his body doubled over in a crouch, his sixgun leveled to make his last bullet count.

No gunfire came. No sound nearby except his own breathing and the heavy wheezing of Goodlove crouched down alongside of him.

Murfee started to go further into the alley slowly, almost at a crawl, intending to fire the instant he caught a sound. He could hear only the yells and shouts that came from the residential section, and shouts behind him at Four Corners. He had moved barely five feet, then tripped over a body.

He swung with his right hand to smash the sixgun's barrel down onto the man's head. He stopped with the weapon in midair. The body didn't move.

Murfee leaned over the man. It was Calem Torrey, lying on his side, a carbine still gripped in his hands. Murfee felt along Torrey's head, and his fingers became slippery with blood. The earth under the dead man's head was damp from a gaping wound above his right ear. Goodlove left Murfee and hurried back along the alleyway toward the street. Murfee paused long enough to double-check to be certain Torrey was dead. Torrey had been hit and had turned to run and escape, but he hadn't traveled more than two strides before he died.

Murfee straightened, thinking of Slattery and Judy Fiske and Ben Shepperd lying in front of the jail. He wiped the wetness from his fingers onto his Levi's and ran as fast as he could from the alley into the street.

CHAPTER TEN

Kneeling in the dust of the street, Augustin Vierra held down the shudder of emotion which made it impossible for him to understand what was being said around him. He could hear whispering and low talk, people questioning if Slattery was still alive and asking about Ben Shepperd and Judy Fiske. Vierra pressed at the wound in Slattery's neck, knowing he must stop the flow of blood or Slattery would die. He knew, lying less than twenty feet from them, Lottie Wells and the storekeeper named Blumberg worked as hard to keep Judy alive. And he knew Sheriff Shepperd was dead. The lawman was dead, and Thomãs, too, who had been cut down with him, might die. The Mexican's long fingers tightened even more above Slattery's collarbone. Blood no longer flowed as freely from the wound, but no matter how hard his fingers pressed, he could not seem to stop the warm seepage.

'Open up! Let me through!' Murfee shouted. He grabbed a few men from behind and hurled them out of his way. One man cursed at the rough treatment, and Augustin wondered why, at a time like this. Murfee knelt beside him. Vierra stared into the cowhand's hard-jawed face. 'The bleeding,' he said. 'It will not stop.'

Murfee took off his hat and laid his head on Slattery's chest. He could not sense a heartbeat. He looked up. 'Move back!' he yelled at the crowd. 'Move back, get back! Give him some air!' He lowered his head again, took hold of Slattery's motionless hand and held it.

Augustin said, 'The blood still seeps.'

Murfee touched the Mexican's arm, silencing him. His fingers pressed the vein at the wrist. 'There's a pulse,' he said. 'There is. I can feel it.' He stood and shoved the nearest onlooker back with both of his hands. 'Back! Move back, so's he can breathe!'

The people moved, edging backwards toward the sides of the street. Mal Weaver had run into Blumberg's store. The crowd opened a path for him as he waved the bandages he held high above his head and called to Murfee. 'Use these! I got enough for Tom and Judy!' He handed half of the bandages to Murfee and continued on to the storekeeper and Judy Fiske.

Murfee folded the top bandage and pressed it against Slattery's neck. Vierra unraveled more of the white cloth to wrap it around the top of the shoulder and side of the neck to completely cover the wound.

Murfee watched Slattery's lips and throat. He could see no sign that Slattery breathed, no perceptive rise and fall of the chest or flutter of the throat. The confused excitement of the conversation all along the roadway was just a jumble of words. He saw four men lift Ben Shepperd to carry him into his office. He didn't know how badly Judy was hurt, only that those who watched Lottie and Blumberg trying to save her hardly spoke a word, and what they did say was spoken in hushed, guarded whispers.

*   *   *

'I saw him. I was goin' into the saloon and I heard the shootin' start,' a man was telling those at the rear of the crowd. 'He hit Slattery and Ben Shepperd 'fore they had a chance.'

'Stinkin' rotten bastard,' another said. 'Nothin' rottener than a bushwhacker. He got what he deserved.'

'He cut that woman down too,' the first speaker added. 'She was runnin' to help Slattery. That's the way it's goin' to be, shootin' a woman like that, how safe are any of us? Or our families?'

Ralph Goodlove watched and listened to the men and women, and also to the talk and reaction of the children. He had taken part in the gunfight. He expected the people would remember, after their excitement calmed. If he'd had a shot at Calem Torrey, he would have killed him. It was the only action he could take, knowing the people were bound to talk about the killings for days, everyone remembering where he or she was when the shooting started, what each saw how he felt.

There would be hate, especially after the sheriff and a woman were killed. That was why he had ordered Torrey to wait at the bridge, not where everyone would be a part of the shooting. He had expected shock, and hate, yet he was not prepared for the way three of the town men dragged Torrey's body by the legs from the dark alleyway and threw him into the street for every man, woman, and child to see. He heard swearing and curses, felt the hate building and building while the onlookers watched Ben Shepperd being carried into the jail. Disgust was mixed with anger and hate of those watching Blumberg and one of the Texas women try to keep Slattery's woman alive. He'd never wanted her shot. Such a beautiful woman. Such a waste.

Murfee, the deputy's badge on his chest shining silver in the lamplight, straightened beside Slattery's body. 'Lift him easy,' he said to Augustin and Mal Weaver. 'Move him careful or that neck wound will open again.'

Goodlove said to Murfee, 'Two of my men are here.' He motioned at Dancer and Waco Jones. 'They'll help.'

'No they won't!' Murfee pointed at Goodlove and then the two cowhands. 'You keep your distance! All of you keep away! That's all!'

Goodlove shook his head. He turned from Murfee, from Vierra and Weaver carrying Slattery, to the people still crowded around Judy Fiske. 'You can't hold me responsible for this.' He looked at Torrey's body. 'I don't know what made Calem go crazy. I went after him with Weaver. I backed the law.'

'And you damn well will back it,' Murfee told him. 'Don't you worry 'bout the law. I'm deputy till an election is held, and you and them hands of yours and everyone else'll do what the law says.'

Murfee walked away from the rancher and followed Weaver and Vierra onto the boardwalk. Both men very careful not to open Slattery's neck wound.

'The first cell,' Murfee told them. 'Put him down easy.'

One of the town men ran from the general store carrying an armful of blankets. The crowd around Judy Fiske opened to let him through. Myron Blumberg took the blankets and spread them on the ground. Then he and three town men gently lifted her onto the makeshift stretcher. The watchers grew quieter, as though holding their breaths would in some way help the badly wounded woman.

'Slow. Walk slowly,' Lottie Wells said to the men. She supported Judy's back, keeping her spine rigid. 'Careful. Careful.'

A low barely audible moan came from Judy's lips. Her eyes were open and she stared glassily at the black night above the faces that helped her.

'She's got to have a doctor,' a woman said. 'Hit in the back like that.'

'She's right,' a man agreed. 'Only a doctor should touch that bullet. Only a doctor can get it out.'

John Hebert a small, white-haired, long-nosed old man with a thin roosterish head looked across his shoulder toward Goodlove. He had been Yellowstone City's blacksmith since the Calligan Valley was first settled. He swore in a high, rasping voice. 'You see what your man did?' he asked the rancher. 'See! They're dead! Ben, and maybe Slattery inside there! And she'll die, too!'

Hebert's wife, as old and thin and chickenlike as her husband, pressed in close to Goodlove. 'You knew there'd be trouble! After your men tried to drag that Mexican. Any one of us could've been shot! Any one of us!'

A growl of agreement sifted through the crowd. Goodlove nodded, trying another approach to the people. 'I don't know what Slattery did to make Torrey go after him. Calem came from Texas. Maybe . . .' His voice broke off. He moved quickly to catch up with Blumberg.

'She'll need a place to stay,' he offered to the storekeeper. 'I'll have Marsh Churchill come to my ranch. She can stay in his house, and Marsh's wife will take care of her.'

'She's being put in the room over my store,' Blumberg answered. Both men looked at Judy. Her eyes were still open, staring at them hazily, as though she could hear their talk through her pain.

Goodlove walked beside Blumberg. He glanced around at the onlookers and raised his voice so everyone could hear. 'I'm sorry about this. I am. Terribly, terribly sorry. She needs a doctor. I'll get a doctor.'

'Mr. Goodlove,' Blumberg said tiredly, 'the

97

nearest doctor is in Bozeman.'

'I'll have one of my men ride to get the doctor from Bozeman and bring him out here.' Goodlove's words were filled with emotion. 'Torrey worked for me and I do have a responsibility in this. I'll pay the doctor to come. I don't care how much it costs.' He swung around and called to Dancer. 'Start riding, Jim. Right now. Get the doctor. Jones, you go with him. Bring the doctor back with you.'

A woman near the bottom porch step said, 'Well, he is trying to do all he can.' Myron Blumberg heard the remark as clearly as Goodlove. Others near them heard it, Goodlove knew, and they quieted, each watcher aware that Jim Dancer had already started to lead Waco Jones down the alleyway to get their horses.

Goodlove realized no real change had taken place in the people. Yet the drone of the voices and the eruptions of angry, hateful talk had calmed some. He had started to swing the attitudes, and he would, knowing how people let other's troubles slip into the backs of their minds, as long as it didn't happen to them.

Goodlove trailed Blumberg across the store porch. The rancher opened the screen door and held it for the men to move through with their burden. 'I'll stay in town myself,' he said to the storekeeper. 'It there's anything else I can do to help, I will. You call on me. I want you to be sure to call me, Myron.'

CHAPTER ELEVEN

Slattery opened his eyes. His first awareness was of a cold dampness around him, a chill that despite the blankets which covered him was part of the ache and pain in his neck and shoulder. He smelled a stale odor of burned coal oil. The smell of tobacco smoke was as stale and heady. The flame in the wall-bracket lamp above him threw a shadowy light that blurred his eyes. Dark thin lines to his right gradually grew longer and longer, and he finally recognized the lines as the iron bars of a cell. He lay in a jail cell, on its hard bunk mattress. He had awakened at other times and had heard voices, far off voices. He'd awakened many times, how many times he didn't know, and he was too tired to think about it . . .

His mind cleared slowly while he dozed and woke at intervals that seemed long and drawn out. Each time he opened his eyes, the smells, lamplight, and bars became clearer. And, gradually, he remembered . . .

He moved his head. Pain, like the jab and slice of a hot blade, slashed down his neck into his right shoulder. He groaned. He tried to stifle another but it came with his breathing,

99

and even that hurt.

Something, a chair, a man's boots, creaked near him. Footsteps sounded, and Augustin Vierra's face stared down at him.

'Thomãs?' Augustin said.

Slattery coughed, feeling the pain dig deep into his neck. Augustin moved away from him and said to someone else in the cell block, 'Get the doctor.'

Slattery whispered, 'Wwwater.'

Augustin poured water from a jug into a tin cup. Then, easily, tenderly, he raised Slattery's head and held the cup to his lips. Slattery coughed as he sipped, but he was able to swallow.

Slattery looked up at Augustin. 'What . . . what happened?'

'Lie still, Thomãs. The doctor will come. He will ease the pain.'

'Judy . . . how's . . . Judy?'

'Judy will be better. She is stronger than you. You have had a hard time these weeks. Rest until the doctor comes.'

Slattery's mind clouded. The pain was lessening. 'Weeks?'

'Three weeks, Thomãs, almost four. But you will be better. Rest.' The soft voice with the Mexican accent faded until it was barely audible, and Slattery felt the blackness of sleep again come over him.

*　　　*　　　*

The feeling of cold and dampness wasn't in the air the next time Slattery became conscious. He lay still and quiet, hearing talk near him. When he opened his eyes, he saw Steve Murfee and Mal Weaver with Augustin. His head ached. Pain sliced into his neck and shoulder when he tilted his head to look at the three men who stood together talking quietly beyond the iron-barred doorway. The other two jail cells were empty. The sheriff's office, like the cell block, was white plaster from the stone floor to the log roof. Slattery had a vague idea something was missing, yet he could not think of what it was. He was trying to clear up in his mind what was wrong in the office and jail, when he saw Murfee glance across his shoulder at him. Murfee spoke to Augustin. The Mexican left the office, and Murfee and Weaver walked into the cell block.

Murfee stared worriedly at Slattery. Then he gave a small grin. 'You sure know how to sleep. How are you feelin'?'

'M' mouth is dry. Water.'

Murfee took the tin cup from the small table that had been placed alongside the bunk. He still wore his deputy's badge. Augustin had worn a badge too. Slattery lay motionless while his head was raised for him to drink. The wetness was good, cool in his dry mouth, trickling through his throat into his body. Pain shot across his shoulder while Murfee returned his head to the pillow. Slattery's mind was hazy. He looked at Weaver and asked, 'How are things?'

Weaver's face was deeply lined. 'Fine. Fine, Tom. We're all out on our own land now. We've started to build. Goodlove's got a sawmill on his spread and he's helped us all. We—'

'Shepperd?' Slattery questioned, realizing who had been missing every time he'd opened his eyes or had been given water or fed. Ben Shepperd hadn't been in his office or the jail. 'Where's the sheriff?'

'He was killed, Tom,' Weaver told him. 'He was shot with you, and he was killed.'

The ache filled Slattery's head, tore at the ligaments of his neck. He lay without speaking, thinking of the lawman, of how the sheriff had backed him, and that now he was dead. He turned his face and looked directly at Murfee. 'Goodlove?' he asked. 'How's he been helpin'?'

'Look, Tom. You had a bad time. Don't press yourself. You're lucky you're alive.'

Slattery's stare switched to Weaver. 'How, Mal?'

Weaver glanced at Murfee, and Murfee shrugged his wide shoulders. Weaver said, 'Goodlove's done nothin' but help every homesteader since you were shot. His hired bands are helpin' us build our shacks and barns, and dig our wells. He's used his wagons to get our hay into the mows for the winter. He's even raised his price two dollars a head for cattle.'

'Is anyone sellin' to him?'

'Some are, some aren't. But he hasn't done one wrong thing, not one thing.' He stepped closer to Slattery's bunk and added hopefully, 'Your section is all set, Tom. The papers are waitin' for you to sign. Judy's already had hers filled out and signed. Fact is, Goodlove's havin' his men put up a house for her.'

'Then she's all right?'

Weaver did not answer. He turned to Murfee, who slowly nodded his head. 'Judy's hurt, but she's gettin' better,' Murfee explained. 'Lottie's been takin' good care of her.' He paused as though he didn't want to continue. His voice was quieter, but stiff and controlled. 'Tom, the doctor Goodlove got from Bozeman had to take a bullet out of Judy's back. She's gettin' better, but there's a good chance she won't walk. She's at Blumberg's.'

'At Blumberg's—' Slattery raised his head from the pillow. Murfee bent over to help him, but it wasn't necessary. The movement of Slattery's head caused too much pain. He lay back, grimacing, breathing heavily. 'She's that bad, Steve? That bad?'

Murfee neither shook his head nor nodded. 'Doc Hobson'll tell you, Tom. He'll stop in, and he'll tell you.'

'I've done about all I can for you,' Doctor John Hobson said to Judy Fiske. He was thirty-four, six years out of Tufts Medical College, a tall, gangling man dressed in a conservative brown suit and a spotless white shirt and collar. Until the day Dancer had come to his Bozeman office, he had never heard of Calligan Valley. After three weeks of living in Yellowstone City, he liked the valley well enough to decide he would move his practice there. He liked this fine young woman in the bed who never complained despite all her discomfort and pain, and Lottie Wells, who had stayed with Judy every minute and had cared for her as well as any nurse. And he marveled at the strength and stamina of Slattery across the street in the jail, so badly hurt that even as a doctor he had not fully believed the man would live out the first week after he had been wounded.

Yet both the man and the woman would live, and John Hobson had made his decision. He did not understand the hate and violence that had been behind the shootout which had caused so much agony and pain. Two men had died, the sheriff of Yellowstone City and the bushwacker.

Hobson had heard talk against Ralph Goodlove when he had arrived, but the talk

104

had toned down and almost stopped as time passed. Goodlove had explained the shooting to him, logically, telling him how shocked he had been himself when his cowhand had gone wild. Goodlove had done so much for Judy Fiske, paying every cent of her expenses, visiting her every day. Hobson mulled this over while he closed his black bag and secured the buckle. He would be happy here. He could build up a practice, and someday, possibly, he would marry and raise his own children. He would go back to Bozeman now. He would close his office there and return to this valley before the winter set in.

Hobson glanced at Augustin Vierra waiting in the bedroom doorway. 'Was he able to talk?' he asked the Mexican. 'Is he that strong?'

'He appears stronger. I think you should examine him.'

'Doctor,' Judy Fiske said, 'can Tom come over here and visit?'

Hobson laughed. 'Not so fast. Not so fast.' His eyes met Lottie Wells', telling her to keep Judy calm. 'He'll need two or three more days to get his strength. Judy, you're stronger than he is.'

Judy did not answer. Hobson paused at the foot of her bed. 'You've got to try to sit.' He again glanced at Lottie. 'We'll try again this afternoon, after she sleeps.' He walked to the door. Judy watched the doctor and then Vierra. 'Augustin,' she asked, 'will you stay a few minutes?'

'I will.' He closed the door behind the doctor. He nodded to Lottie Wells. 'Unless you think she's too tired.'

'She can talk a little while,' Lottie told him. 'If only she would try to sit.'

'How is Tom?' Judy asked. 'The truth, Augustin.'

'He's coming along well. Very well. He will be over to see you soon as he is able to get up and walk.'

Judy stared into the Mexican's dark eyes. 'Does he know about this?' She nodded her head, slowly, at her motionless body beneath the blankets. 'Does he?'

'It would not mean one thing to him. You know Thomãs better than that.'

Judy was silent, and into the quiet Lottie Wells said, 'She has been awake a long while. I think she should sleep.'

Nodding, Augustin back-stepped toward the door. Judy did appear tired and drawn, he thought. Possibly it was the time of the year, her recovery of strength slowed by the chilly nights of fall. The weather did not stay warm during this time of year and then change gradually like in the south of Texas or in his own home in Mexico, but almost overnight the cold and threat of snow could be felt. Myron Blumberg had had a small wood stove moved into the room from the store, yet the heat given off by the burned wood did not fully

106

drive out the cold. That, and the fact Judy could not move her legs, could slow her recovery. Augustin smiled at her. 'I'll be in tonight to tell you of Thomãs.'

'Tell him I'll be waiting for him.'

'I will. Yes, I will tell him.' He revolved the knob and went into the hallway. He was glad to be out of the room. It was not that he failed to enjoy each visit with Judy. He felt about her and Thomãs Slattery as though they were one. But there was something he could sense in her manner the past weeks, a different kind of quietness she had not shown before she had been shot. She seemed by her talk and actions to be completely alone, even though others were in the room.

He paused at the top of the stairs. Looking down into the long wide store he could see Blumberg was busy at the coffee grinder, and that Ralph Goodlove had opened the porch screen door and now walked past the counters of the middle aisle. Augustin started down the stairs, his face serious. No matter how much Goodlove tried to do, bringing the doctor to help Judy and Thomãs, offering more money for cattle, helping in the building of the new ranch houses and barns, Augustin could not help believe there was more than what could be seen to the rancher's actions.

Goodlove's handsome face was as serious as Augustin's. He halted on the bottom step to allow the Mexican to pass him. 'How is Miss

Fiske today?' he asked.

Vierra shook his head. 'The doctor has done all he can. But I do not know. She is so quiet.'

Goodlove nodded. 'She'd naturally be quiet. She's been made to stay inside that room too long. When she gets into her own home, she'll pick up.'

'Your men have completed her house?'

'Almost.' He smiled, happy with his news. 'The kitchen and bedroom have been finished. And the barn is almost done.' He moved past Vierra, and then he halted. 'I've sent to Bozeman for a stove that is big enough to throw enough heat to keep out the cold all winter.' He gazed toward the landing and the closed bedroom door. His eyes returned to the Mexican. 'Could you ask Weaver to bring his wagon out front. The doctor said we can move her today. We'd better be sure she is settled in her own home before the snow starts.'

Vierra nodded. 'I will be with Weaver's wagon. We will move her.'

Goodlove shook his head. 'You don't have to help. Torrey rode for me. I want to do all I can for her. And for Slattery, if he'll let me.' He did not wait for an answer, simply continued up the stairs and knocked on the bedroom door.

Lottie opened the door. When she saw who had knocked, she kept her hand on the knob. 'Judy's trying to sleep,' she said, brushing a

108

stray strand of dark hair away from her forehead. Her face didn't show even a trace of a smile. 'She needs to rest.'

'I'll only stay a moment,' the rancher said. He stepped forward and went past her.

Judy watched the doorway, as though she waited to see him. He felt the same warm sense of calm he always felt when he saw her. The doctor had little hope she would walk again, but Goodlove did not agree. This woman was the only woman he had ever wanted in his lifetime. He had so much now and would own every acre of any worth in the valley before he was through. Judy, even without the use of her legs, had the strength to match his. He said, 'The doctor thinks it will be all right to move you. Your house is ready. Mal Weaver will have his wagon out front later today.'

Lottie said, 'She can't go now. Not in a wagon.'

'It's either that or take a chance on being locked in this room for the winter. One rain storm and the road will rut. It will be far more uncomfortable moving her then. And more dangerous.' He stepped closer to the iron posts of the bed and looked down at Judy. 'A snowstorm could blow down from Canada at any time. You'd be stuck here all winter.'

'She won't be stuck here alone,' Lottie began, then Judy interrupted.

'I'd like to stay long enough to talk to Tom,'

she said to Goodlove. 'It isn't that I don't appreciate what you've done, but I want to see him.'

'I can arrange that.' He smiled, calm and understanding. 'You'll feel much more at home in your own house.' He turned to Lottie. 'A room has been furnished for you to stay with her.'

'I'll go out there, don't you worry,' Lottie answered. The distaste she had for Goodlove was clear in her face as she looked at Judy and added, 'I still believe you'd do better to wait. Another day or two.'

'No,' Judy said. 'It's better this way. I can't live in Myron's home all winter.' She nodded to Goodlove. 'Thank you, Ralph.'

Goodlove left the room. Closing the door behind him, he paused in the hallway. Lottie's words came through the thin wood. 'I think you're wrong,' she was saying. 'You shouldn't trust that man.' Judy did not answer, and Goodlove descended the staircase. The fact that Judy had not agreed with Lottie was enough for the present. What Lottie thought, or what Vierra or Blumberg thought, did not matter.

He had seen how cold and matter-of-fact the Mexican had been, and how the storekeeper had kept busy grinding coffee and had not as much as nodded to him when he'd entered. Now Blumberg continued to keep his attention on the coffee grinder, showing he did not want to talk. Goodlove walked past the storekeeper, pushed open the screen door, and stepped out onto the porch. Blumberg, Lottie Wells, the Mexican, each could do all the thinking and talking he wanted, and he would still have his way. He had almost lost the townspeople after the gunfight, but he had made every effort he could to help Judy and Slattery, and he had changed the distrust to respect. His taking Judy to her home couldn't be stopped. Water had frozen in the ranch buckets last night. The jagged peaks of the Gallatins and Madisons to the north showed large stretches of white where the mountain storms had been leaving snow. Everyone in the valley had seen how the snow line crawled down lower and lower.

Goodlove walked slowly while he crossed Four Corners. He would have the doctor pass Judy's words on to Slattery. He wasn't taking one chance that she could think he had failed to do his best for her in every way. After Slattery was dead, he wanted Judy to remember he had done all he could for her. And Slattery would die. There would be no Goodlove Valley while Slattery lived. There would be no Judith Goodlove.

He thought of Slattery lying on the cell bunk, his body still weak from loss of blood. With Judy at her ranch, Slattery would certainly go out to visit her. He wouldn't be as strong or as careful as he had to be. Goodlove

111

glanced once more toward the snow-topped peaks. His eyes were narrowed, his face wooden. He knew exactly how he would have Slattery taken care of, and at last, he nodded.

CHAPTER TWELVE

Slattery leaned back from the edge of the cell bunk. He sweated after the effort of pulling on his boots, and a quick pulsebeat throbbed in his neck. Getting into his shirt and Levi's had been easy for him. Now he needed a few minutes rest to catch his breath. He sat without moving until the pulsebeat calmed and he no longer felt the breathless pressure in his chest.

Steve Murfee said from the cellblock doorway, 'Maybe you'd better wait. Two or three more days, you'll be able to have someone drive you out to see her.'

'I'm all right,' Slattery answered testily. He'd been able to get up onto his feet at noon, but he had been forced to lie down because of his weakness. An hour later, he'd tried again and had taken a few shaky steps. He exhaled slowly, and his breathing calmed. 'I'll only be out there a few minutes. I can make it.'

'I still think you ought to wait. Remember, the doc said you'd be weak and shaky.'

'Look, Steve, just hand me the coat. I want

to see Judy. I want to talk to her.'

Murfee walked into the office to get Slattery's sheepskin coat. Slattery leaned forward. Carefully, he set his weight on both of his feet and stood. He'd believed he'd have plenty of time to get stronger before he'd try to go across into Blumberg's store and talk with Judy. He'd believed she would do better to stay in town until she was stronger, but then he'd thought about her decision to go to her ranch and had understood. Lottie would stay in her house and take care of her. Two of the men who'd made the cattle drive with them from Texas had offered to help her. Lute Canby was as fine a ranchhand as Slattery had ever known, as was Running Bear, the Comanche who had handled the remuda on the long trip north.

He gripped the iron bars for support and moved into the office. Weaver waited on the boardwalk. The bearded homesteader looked in through the doorway. 'They're carryin' her down,' he told Slattery. He stepped inside while Murfee held Slattery's coat.

The street was deeply shadowed in the late afternoon. A sharp chill filled the air. He remembered the day had been very warm when he and Judy had been shot. And Ben Shepperd killed. Slattery could not stop thinking about Shepperd, and that the trouble hadn't really ended because a man like Goodlove didn't make changes as clean-cut as

113

the changes of season in this north country. Winter's cold rode on the grayish, heavy clouds that had rolled up around the Galatins and Madisons. Judy was right to get settled in her house before the snows started.

Slattery looked away from the snow line on the huge, cloud-hazy granite peaks to Weaver's canvas covered carreta. Lute Canby, his bald head hatless, supported the front of the stretcher which held Judy. Running Bear carried the other end. Lottie Wells and Myron Blumberg stood near the tailgate with Nancy Weaver. Goodlove waited in the middle of the street. His back was turned to the jail during the time it took the two cowmen to move down the porch steps and carefully slide the stretcher onto the wagon bed.

When Slattery crossed the street, Goodlove moved aside with the few townspeople who had stopped to watch. Judy's head was turned toward Slattery and Murfee walking close behind him. She smiled up at Slattery.

'Tom, I'm so glad. I wanted to see you before I left.'

'I'll be riding out,' he told her. 'In a day or two.'

'Not so soon,' she said. He leaned over and looked into her face, feeling his dizziness and shakiness. 'I'll be out. We have a lot to talk about.'

Her eyes closed. Then she opened them again and smiled. 'Yes, we will talk. Be sure you are well enough to ride.'

Murfee said, 'Okay, Mal, better get started.' He held Lottie's arm while she climbed onto the wagon seat. He stood alongside Slattery and watched Weaver jiggle the reins to start the mule team slowly along the roadway.

The onlookers moved off toward the walks and buildings. Running Bear, dressed in a cowhand's checkered shirt and jeans, touched Slattery's arm. 'We'll take good care of her,' he said. Canby nodded, his whiskered face serious. 'Come out soon as you're able,' he added. 'Judy'll be all right. You jest take care of y'self, Tom.'

Slattery's legs were weak, his stomach woozy, and he realized the truth of the doctor's warning about not trying to stay on his feet too long. He had wanted to say so much more to Judy, but his mind wasn't clear, and what he would say wasn't for everyone in Yellowstone City to hear. He watched the wagon roll past the buildings to the west. There was so much more he wanted to say to her, so much more.

His weakness made him shakier as he turned to start back across the street, and he stumbled. Murfee moved quickly to grab hold of him. Goodlove, closer to Slattery, reached out and gripped his arm. Slattery regained his footing and pulled away from him.

'I'm all right,' Slattery snapped, glaring into the rancher's face. 'I don't need your help. I

115

don't want anything from you.'

Goodlove dropped his hand. 'I was only trying to help,' he said. Those on the deeply shadowed walks and porches were frozen where they stood. The rancher glanced at them, then continued in a louder tone, 'I've tried to do all I could to help. I've tried to explain—'

'You still have to explain about Ian Huffaker and Fred McDonald!' Slattery wavered on his heels, but wouldn't allow Murfee to help him. 'You'll have to come up with an answer about them!'

'I already have explained all I know,' the rancher said. 'I have tried, the people know I have done all I could, and I'm still trying.' He backed away from Slattery and walked to his horse. He moved quickly, making it clear to the watchers he wanted to leave before more trouble could start.

Slattery watched Goodlove mount his stallion and follow the carreta westward. He realized he had won nothing. He'd only let the people of Yellowstone City know how he felt. He walked toward the jail, taking slow and careful steps.

Donald Ketchuck from the government land bureau hurried from the doorway of his office to meet Slattery on the boardwalk. Ketchuck said, 'You were wrong, Mr. Slattery. Dancer was cleared of any connection to your men.'

116

'No, I'm not wrong. Goodlove will answer for his men.'

The agent's thin face was sure, serious, while he nodded. 'He's trying to make up for what Torrey did. Can't you see that? He's even come into my office and helped Mrs. Huffaker straighten out her papers.'

'That isn't enough,' Slattery said. 'Not for me, it isn't.' He continued across the walk into the jail, angry at himself for giving the townspeople reason to side with Goodlove. He felt he'd let Judy down too. He'd wanted to say so much to her, and they'd said almost nothing. He was so weak and tired. He hadn't helped Judy and, thinking of the land agent's words, he wasn't certain how much he had lost in his battle with Goodlove. He was certain only that Goodlove would push trouble when he was ready for it. As long as he was alive, Goodlove had to work against him, and trouble would come . . .

*   *   *

The trouble came sooner than Slattery expected.

He returned to the cell bunk and remained there all night. The thick black clouds that had boiled up over the Gallatins and Madisons covered the entire valley by midnight, and the range had its first snow. The wind's low moan raised in pitch, slapping hard at the walls and doors, plastering the snow icily over the windows. Augustin kept the jail's potbelly stove filled with cottonwood logs, and he and Murfee stayed up most of the night talking with Slattery.

They told him about everything that Goodlove had done since the shootout, his constant attention to Judy, the hiring of the doctor to care for her and for Slattery himself, the help and advice the rancher had personally given to every Texan who had hastily thrown up a shack and barn for protection against the high-country winter. The rancher hadn't tried to have Murfee removed from the temporary sheriff's job, nor Augustin changed as deputy. Goodlove had been the picture of good intentions, right down to taking Judy to her ranchhouse in Weaver's wagon.

'He's even been lendin' out his riders to help get hay into the barns,' Steve Murfee said. 'Goodlove's given wire to those who want their hay baled. He hasn't asked one thing for himself. He even paid two dollars more a head for the beeves he's bought.'

'How many has he taken?' asked Slattery.

'More than fifteen—maybe sixteen-hundred head. Some of the other ranchers have bought about five hundred. That spreads them out wide over the range.'

Slattery thought about everything while he lay back and closed his eyes to sleep. He could remember only snatches of the talk he had

118

heard in the alternate periods of waking and sleeping during the past three weeks. Goodlove had made visits to learn how he improved. The rancher had stayed near the doctor, visiting Judy each day. He had stayed at Churchill's house to be close, to help, so the people could see how he tried to make up for Torrey's bushwhacking. Slattery understood exactly how much more strength Goodlove had gained because of the gunfight. The land agent's trust in him was clear enough. Even Judy had to give the man credit for seeing she was personally taken care of by the only doctor in the Territory.

The wind outside grew in violence toward morning, beating with an abrasive grind against the glass with wild gusty screams before it rent its fury over the southern cliffs. The storm blowing down from Canada, unseasonal and unpredictable, could mean a long bad stretch that would be extra rough on the Texans and their Longhorns which were already tired and worn from the long trail drive and drought.

The snow did not let up until the morning of the second day. Slattery moved around the office. He continually talked to Murfee or Augustin, except when they left to make their rounds of the town. The lone visitor to the jail was Myron Blumberg who brought in a warm bearskin coat for Slattery. Slattery felt stronger. He stood for long periods of time at the window and stared out through the ice-covered glass, watching the powdery, shifting whiteness build gradually into deepening drifts along the roadway, walks, and porches of the buildings fronting Four Corners. On the second morning he saw his first sleigh, the general store open wagon set on high iron runners for Blumberg's delivery boy to reach the nearest ranches.

Color had returned to Slattery's face after two days of being on his feet. His periods of tiredness were less frequent. His headaches and the jabs of pain that slid down from his neck and shoulder into his chest came only when he moved or turned too quickly. The wind slackened, the snow gradually stopped falling, and by afternoon the sun showed bright and dazzling through small breaks in the clouds.

Slattery waited another day, until the walks had been dug out and Myron Blumberg's sleigh, using two large thick boards attached below the driver's seat, plowed the street. Then he went across to the store and borrowed the storekeeper's bay mare and sleigh to drive to Judy Fiske's new home.

'You're not goin' out alone?' Steve Murfee said the next morning when Slattery was putting on a second pair of Levi's. 'That's a good five miles.'

'The sleigh'll make it easy enough.' Slattery chose a long-barrelled .73 Winchester from the wall rack. He checked its load and tucked it under his arm.

Murfee stood without moving, watching Slattery carefully make his way across the white-covered intersection toward the general store. He knew there was no use in arguing with Slattery. He had made up his mind about going. But his taking a carbine along meant he expected that sooner or later Goodlove would come after him.

Steve Murfee stepped back from the office window and looked past the iron cell block to where Augustin was putting fresh logs into the stove. 'Take over, Gus,' he said. 'I'm saddlin' up and goin' out with Tom.'

*　　*　　*

'That's John Colburn's place,' Murfee said when they passed the first house built two miles from town, south of the river.

Chimney smoke from Colburn's fireplace had been visible above the river timber for the last ten minutes. The thin dark column rose straight up, etching a hazy line against the clear blue sky and the eye-blinking brightness of the sun. In most spots the snow's depth was little more than a foot, but the drifts were three or four feet deep. Cattle grazed on patches where the wind had swept the grass clean. Slattery circled the sleigh around a small meadowlike area close to the river's high north bank. The half day of warm sun had melted most of the snow along the stream edge, and the depth and rush of water covered all trace of sandbars. Turning the horse again into the roadway, Slattery could see the Colburn homestead clearer. The house was a small two-room shack, the barn behind it twice the size of the house.

'How many head did John keep?' he asked Murfee.

'Ten, I think. That's all he and his old woman can handle. They built this close to town so they wouldn't have far to travel.'

Slattery nodded, thoughtfully, feeling something wasn't right on Colburn's homestead yet not quite certain what he found strange about how the house and barn had been built. The trees ahead, the cottonwood limbs and willows and thick brush, a forest of white from the storm, opened onto a wooden bridge. Murfee started his buckskin across. The sleigh slid along smoothly behind the horses, the runners making a sweeping sound over the new-fallen snow.

The sudden collapse of the bridge came as a complete shock. Murfee's horse moved past the midsection, lifting its hoofs carefully not to stumble or slip. Blumberg's bay mare was in stride five feet behind the buckskin, the sleigh gliding along smoothly on its shiny runners. The bridge timbers suddenly creaked under the weight of the rider and both horses and the sleigh and driver. The supports snapped, then broke completely, and the thick heavy planking began to crumble and drop toward the water.

Murfee spurred his buckskin onto the solid section of the bridge, but Slattery did not have time enough to whip the bay mare. He could feel the rear end of the sleigh tilt backwards. The bay mare pulled, kicking its hoofs to escape being dragged down. Slattery's Winchester fell from the seat and dropped, splashing into the water below. The rear of the sleigh hung suspended over the deep, swirling current, the runners slowly slipping back further and further. Blumberg's horse set all four legs into the snow and stood stiff and straining. But the weight of the man and sleigh were clearly too much to hold.

'Don't jump!' Murfee yelled. He'd grabbed his lariat while he'd swung his buckskin. The way the sleigh hung, any attempt by Slattery to shift his weight would dump him into the rushing water. Another minute and the sleigh's weight would pull the horse down with it. 'Catch this line, Tom!' He circled the noose above his head and let it go.

Slattery caught the rope. Standing, holding onto the sleigh's side, he looped the noose around behind the seat, then held on while Murfee pulled the line taut. Slattery stared down into the swirling rush of the blackish-white channel, knowing once he fell he wouldn't have the strength to fight the swift, icy current. 'Pull, Steve! Pull!'

Murfee had his end of the rope snubbed in his saddle horn. The buckskin's hoofs slid on the snow, one inch backward, another. Blumberg's bay had been drawn back closer to the brink. 'Hold! Hold, boy!' Murfee said to the buckskin. 'Hold!'

Slattery grabbed the whip. Off balance, clinging to the seat with his left hand, he lashed out at the bay's flanks. The whip cracked like a gunshot when it struck. The horse slipped back, back, and Slattery swung again.

Murfee's buckskin held now, the lariat stretched so tight the rope threatened to break. Blumberg's bay whinnied wildly, digging its hoofs into the snow. Slattery swung the whip once more. Murfee jabbed with his spurs. Both animals strained with every ounce of their strength. The sleigh stopped slipping. It hung without motion for a few seconds, and then began to inch forward.

Slattery threw the whip onto the leather seat. He gripped the side and held firm, leaning forward while the sleigh slowly moved up onto the solid planking. Murfee's horse pulled. The wagon mare, still terrified, strained to get off the bridge as fast as possible, and the sleigh slid ahead quickly.

Slattery slowed the vehicle, then stopped the frightened horse. Sharp stabs of pain

124

thrust down through his neck and shoulder into his chest. He sat without moving to catch his breath and let the throbbing calm.

Murfee swung off his buckskin and hurried to Slattery's side. When he reached up to help Slattery stand, Slattery said, 'No, wait. Give me time. I need time.'

Nodding, Murfee walked through the snow to the edge of the river bank. The logs which had broken free had been washed downstream. If Slattery had been alone, he would have gone under with the sleigh and horse. He wouldn't have stood a chance. Murfee studied the piling that had held the collapsed section of bridge. The thick timber was barely visible under the rushing white froth. He crouched down, keeping a firm footing so he wouldn't slip, and strained to see the broken supports.

'Hey! Hey, there!' The high-pitched voice calling from the snow-covered trees was unmistakable. Murfee glanced at old John Colburn hurrying toward them through the deep drifts. Slattery stood and climbed carefully off the step plate.

'Look at that, Tom,' Murfee said. 'Those pilings are sheared off too smooth to have just caved in.'

Slattery stared into the deep rush of the channel. He still felt wobbly. That sensation calmed when he could see the tops of the pilings. Four heavy timbers had been driven deep into the riverbed to support the center of the bridge. The break in each support was whitish, so clean-cut only a saw could have done the job.

'It took time to weaken those pilings.' Murfee shook his head. 'How, with the water so deep?'

'I heard you and your horses,' Colburn halted alongside Slattery. The old man's small roosterish body was completely hidden by his buffalo-hide coat. 'I was diggin' a path to my barn and heard you.' He looked at Slattery. 'You were lucky. Mighty lucky.' His thin face peered down at the pilings, his bony nose red from the cold. 'I knew them two were up to somethin'! I knew!'

Slattery said, 'What two?'

'I don't know. My woman looked out 'bout an hour ago and saw two men on the other side of the bridge. They left their horses in the woods so they couldn't be seen, but we spotted them.'

Murfee exhaled a long, patient breath that drifted like smoke in front of his face. 'John, you saw them, and you didn't find out what they were up to?'

'Too danged cold. You expect I'd come out? It looked like they was breakin ice 'round them pilin's. I didn't think what else they'd be up to.' His long-nosed face reddened, his anger growing now. 'You're sheriff, Murfee. You don't expect me and my woman'd think this'd happen?' He was going to add more, but Slattery interrupted.

'Will you go into town, John?' he asked. 'Tell Augustin to get a few men out here to do something about this before dark. At least have them put up barriers so no one else will try to cross.'

The small roosterish old man muttered to himself. 'I'll go. I'll go, but you don't blame me! I ain't to blame!'

'We're not blaming you, John. Just tell Augustin.'

Slattery heard Colburn's 'I will' as he turned with Murfee and started away from the river bank. The weakening of the bridge was done to get him, he was certain. His asking to borrow Blumberg's sleigh could have been known by anyone. The shortest way to Judy Fiske's ranch was over this bridge. But those who had sawed the pilings hadn't reckoned on being seen. And their horses' tracks would be clear enough in the snow.

Slattery walked to Murfee's buckskin. He reached up and pulled the Spencer carbine from its scabbard. Habitually, he checked its load.

'You swear me in,' he said to Murfee. 'I want this to be strictly legal.'

CHAPTER THIRTEEN

The tracks of two horses were clear in the snow, but they were lost to Slattery and Murfee before they followed them three-hundred yards.

The men who had weakened the bridge had ridden off the high north bank down to the water's edge. The sandy bottom, built up along both sides of the stream by the downward rush of the water from the mountains, was solid and hard. The riders had held their mounts far enough out in the current so the horses' hoofs left absolutely no trail.

Slattery kept the sleigh close to the willows and cottonwoods and brush that screened the river, while Murfee followed the sandy edges trying to spot a hoofprint or a mark that would show where the riders had gone out of the water. The air had warmed under a bright bluebird sky, bell-clear and with very little wind. Slattery opened the collar of his sheepskin and breathed in the clean, fine air. He felt stronger, better than he had since he had left the cell bunk, despite the soreness in his arms and back muscles from holding onto the sleigh at the bridge.

The drifts off to the southwestern rim were deeper than the snow north of the river. Slattery stayed in the cover of the trees while he approached and passed two small homesteads. Far ahead, he could see a third, much larger ranch which had a big house and huge barn.

No hoofprints could be found. Both Slattery and Murfee knew the riders could have gone either north or south, leaving the water when they were positive they could not be caught.

Murfee rode his buckskin onto the bank. He pulled in alongside the sleigh, brushing his flat-crowned hat and sheepskin free of the snow that had fallen onto him from the willows and cottonwoods. He gestured towards four wagons near the barn and at three cowhands who worked forking hay up through the open door of the barn's mow.

'That's Judy's place,' he told Slattery. His outstretched arm swung behind them and pointed along their backtrail. Forty Longhorns grazing in the spotty, wind-swept meadows were blots of gray and brown against the white. 'The first spread we passed is Mal Weaver's. The next belongs to Sue Huffaker. Between there and Judy's is yours.'

Slattery studied his land. Neither a shack nor barn had been built for him. The cattle bunched together beyond Judy's house and barn numbered about one-hundred head. Judy would have asked that his share of the herd be kept with hers and he could understand why his grass had been cut to be stored in the mow of Judy's barn.

Murfee lowered the brim of his hat and shaded his eyes against the glare of the snow. 'No sense in my goin' huntin alone,' he said. 'I could travel up and down the river all day and not find anythin'.' He gestured at the men and horses and wagons. 'They've been workin' right down to the edge of the stream. Any tracks leavin' the river close to here would be lost too.'

Slattery nodded and swung the sleigh toward the buildings.

The house was three times the size of the Colburns' shack, big and sprawling, with a veranda running the length of its front. Goodlove's men must have worked long, hard hours to build it so fast . . . Slattery stopped thinking about that as soon as he drew close enough to see clearly who directed the men. Any doubt he might have had about the sawed timbers of the bridge also vanished.

'That's Goodlove on the sorrel,' Murfee said. His right hand dropped to the bottom buttons of his heavy coat. He flicked the sheepskin open to expose his holstered .44.

Slattery laid the Spencer carbine flat across his lap. The cattlehands on the wagon nearest him had paused with their pitchforks in their hands to watch them approach. Goodlove shouted at them and they resumed clearing the hay of snow.

Goodlove turned his sorrel stallion toward Slattery and Murfee. Only one of the vehicles behind the rancher was a regular farm wagon. Two of the others were heavy-duty sleighs, the fourth a jumper sleigh. Goodlove waved to Slattery and Murfee.

'Glad to see you're out, Slattery,' he called. 'Judy will be happy to see you.' He grinned at Murfee. 'Sheriff.'

Neither Murfee nor Slattery returned the smile. They rode close to the wagons and stopped. Murfee asked Goodlove, 'Which two of your men haven't been workin' right along with you?'

'What?' Goodlove looked at his cattlehands. The men in the wagons stopped their work. None wore a sixgun outside his coat. The tallest, a heavy, square-faced man with a week's growth of dark black beard, wiped his sweating forehead with his bare hand. The man closest to him, as heavy but shorter and clean-shaven, said, 'Ain't been working? Mister, we been workin' here since sunup. This hay ain't cut and stacked itself.'

Murfee's stare shifted to the mow. Behind Dancer, he could see Dave McPeck, another of the Texans who had made the trail drive. 'Two men weakened the bridge timbers so it'd cave in,' he said bluntly. 'John Colburn saw them. Slattery was almost dumped in with the horse and sleigh. We tracked them into the river.'

Goodlove's handsome features did not change. 'I haven't been to town. My men have been right here all morning.'

'I see Dancer. What about Waco Jones?'

'Sheriff, you've got no right to push my men.'

'Waco Jones,' Murfee repeated. 'Where is he?'

Goodlove shook his head. He was irritated, making a definite effort to control himself. He called up into the mow. 'Dave, tell Jonesie I want him to come out here.'

Dave McPeck motioned understanding and called down to the men who worked at the rear of the barn. Mal Weaver walked along the aisle between the stalls to the open front doorway. He waved and grinned widely. 'Hey, Tom! Steve! Good to see you out, Tom! Danged good!'

Slattery said, 'You been here since Goodlove's hands started?'

'Sure have. Since sunup. We were lucky that storm didn't last any longer and bury all the grass.'

'I thought it would be best to get the barns stocked,' Goodlove explained. Weaver nodded as the rancher continued. 'We're in for a hard winter. I didn't want to lose the grass if the range iced too fast.'

Slattery did not answer. He watched Waco Jones step into the doorway behind Weaver. Jones wore a hip-long woolen coat. His face was flushed and sweating from the work he had been doing.

Goodlove called to him, his voice loud in the sudden quiet of the yard. 'Tell them where you've been all day.'

Jones spat a mouthful of tobacco juice into the snow. He said matter-of-factly, 'Right here inside this barn. Balin' hay.'

'All day?' Slattery questioned. 'Two hours ago?'

Jones again spit onto the muddy snow. His stare locked with Slattery's.

'Look,' he said. 'The boss says I answer his question. Don't you try makin' something out of it.'

Mal Weaver said, 'He's tellin' the truth, Tom. Mr. Goodlove's cowhands began helpin' me cut and store my grass. I've been here all day.' He looked at McPeck. 'So's Dave and Dancer and Jonesie.' He motioned toward the men in the wagons. 'And Neill and La Farge have been workin' too.'

'They didn't leave at all?'

'No. Nobody left.' Weaver nodded to Goodlove. 'Mr. Goodlove knows these Montana winters. Soon's he noticed his horses gettin' their winter coats, he rode around to all our spreads. He helped us finish our barns so's we'd stock plenty of hay.'

Murfee still was doubtful. His lips parted to speak, but Slattery said, 'Let it go, Steve.'

Murfee shook his head. 'Damn it, that bridge was weakened so you'd break through.' He quieted as Slattery raised his hand, and

133

both of them glanced toward the house. Lottie Wells had appeared on the porch from the doorway. She waved to them. Slattery said, 'Mal and Dave say they were here, it's enough for me. Let it go.' He lifted his reins to start the bay. Murfee kneed his buckskin.

Dancer muttered an obscenity. His eyes were narrowed under his sweating forehead. 'I don't like a man callin' me a liar. Anyone feels like pushin' me, let him try it.'

'No, we don't want trouble,' Goodlove snapped. 'Get back to work.'

Dancer made no motion to leave the barn, but his voice carried his hate. 'No one calls me a liar, Mr. Goodlove! I took enough in Yellowstone 'fore Torrey was killed! I don't take no more from that one!' He glared at Slattery in the sleigh moving slowly toward the house. Then his stare shifted to Weaver and McPeck. 'You saw that! You heard him push me! He pushed Jonesie, all of us, talkin' like that.'

Weaver's bearded face was worried. 'He had a close shave. He didn't accuse you of anything.'

'I know what he meant!' Dancer said hotly. 'You do too! Both of you! You remember that sonofabitch pushed us! You damn well remember when the time comes!'

Riding close to Slattery, Murfee said, 'I don't like droppin' it, Tom. Not like that, I don't.'

'Mal and Dave wouldn't cover up for them,' Slattery said. 'Neither would Running Bear or Canby. Goodlove didn't have one of those men do the job. The two who weakened the bridge rode south. They were smart enough to figure we'd continue heading this way, not go south away from Judy's ranch.'

'Akkesson and Magoon built down near the south pass. They could've seen them.'

'Not with the snow and trees giving so much cover. All they had to do was keep to the brush, and they wouldn't be seen. Then they could swing back across the valley floor to Goodlove's.' Slattery looked at Lottie Wells as he drew the mare to a halt. Lottie had stepped to the edge of the porch and waited, smiling at both Slattery and Murfee. She was very pretty, brushing a stray strand of her dark hair away from her forehead. 'We didn't think you'd be out this soon, Tom J,' she said. 'Judy will be so glad to see you.' Her eyes and smile shifted to Murfee, welcoming the tall lawman.

'You shouldn't be out in this cold dressed like that,' Murfee told her, nodding toward her cotton dress. 'Cold's too easy to catch.'

'I just stepped out for a minute.'

'Shouldn't take a chance. You get a cold, Judy'd pick it up.' He dismounted while Slattery stepped carefully down from the seat of the sleigh and then as carefully walked up the porch steps.

Lottie opened the storm door. 'Judy has had

135

a hard time, Tom J,' she said. 'This hasn't been easy for her. It won't get any easier.'

The house was well-built and warm. The huge stone living room fireplace threw the heat into the small front hallway. The single long room which ran the entire length of one side of the house was a combination living room and kitchen. A leather couch and three leather chairs were arranged neatly on the oval braided rug. The kitchen table and chairs were heavy pine, and an inside pump jutted above the enclosed sink. White curtains gave a warm, comfortable feeling to the house. Lottie went to the first of the two side doors and opened it. Judy was propped up, half-seated against three pillows on a thick-quilted bed. She stared past Lottie at Slattery and raised her right hand to him.

'Tom,' she said.

Murfee began to follow Slattery, until Lottie touched his arm. 'I'll make some coffee, Steve. You can help.'

Slattery forgot Steve and Lottie. He entered the room. He'd noted Judy's quiet, serious manner, that she'd not had a trace of smile on her lips. She didn't smile now, while he took off his coat and moved the pine rocker beside the bed. He grinned down at her. 'You look better. That's what you needed. To get out of town.'

'How are you, Tom?'

'Coming along. Little ache here, pain there.'

136

His grin faded. 'What is it, Judy?'

She held her stare on him for a full minute, then switched her eyes to the bedroom doorway. They could hear Lottie and Steve's happy laughter and talk in the kitchen. Her black hair was pulled back and tied with a blue ribbon, giving her lovely face the intent calmness she took on when she was especially grave. To Slattery, she was no thinner, her color was almost as though she had been out in the sun that morning. But something was wrong. She said, 'You'll be all right. I'm so glad you came. I was so worried.' She glanced toward the white-curtained window. The call of a man's voice and the whinny of a horse penetrated the glass. 'I was so worried.'

'I was worried about you. But we're both coming along. And things will be better by next spring.'

'I'll be right here next spring,' she said looking directly at him. 'And the next spring. And the next.'

'Judy?'

'No, Tom. The doctor said I could always be like this.' She was completely under control, yet Slattery caught a tremble of her mouth as she went on. 'You led the people here. You gave them, every family, a chance for a new life. You have a chance for a new life yourself. I'm not going to marry you and spoil that for you.'

'You are going to marry me. What I feel

137

didn't end out in Yellowstone City's street.'

Judy shook her head. 'A man needs a woman who can take care of his home, and his children. Tom, I can't even give you children. Not like this. The doctor said—'

'He said? He didn't really say anything for sure. It's only been a month. Look at you. You can almost sit up. You will be sitting up, and walking. I don't like this, Judy. I'm not letting it end with just talk.'

Judy swallowed and turned away from him. She didn't answer because Lottie and Steve had come into the room, but stared toward the window and listened to the noises of the men and horses outside. Lottie held out a mug of coffee to Slattery. 'Here, you can use this, Tom J.' She glanced at Murfee. 'We can talk, and then I'll make supper.'

Judy said, 'I don't think Tom should be out that long. It will be dark in a few hours. He should get back before the sun goes down.'

Murfee laughed. 'We'll have time. I want to eat some of my girl's good cookin'.'

Slattery said to Lottie, 'We better head back early. There'll be plenty of time for meals out here.' He grinned from Lottie to Murfee, then at Judy. 'You'll have us out here often enough.' He took a mouthful of the hot coffee, swallowed it and felt the good warmth flow down through his throat into his chest. But he saw that Judy hadn't even smiled. Her head was turned on the pillow, facing the window as though she listened only to the sounds outside.

*   *   *

Ralph Goodlove watched the bedroom windows. He knew that Judy often looked out at him and the others he had working for her. He had spent hours sitting with her during the three days she had been inside her house. Twice during the storm he had ridden the seven-mile distance from his ranch with the wind and icy snow whipping and tearing at his face. He had done that so she would realize exactly how much he was willing to go through to visit her. She knew he wanted her. He had written to medical schools and colleges in the East to learn the names of doctors who specialized in her kind of spine injury. Doctor Hobson had set up his practice less than two years ago. He didn't know all the answers. There was hope, and Goodlove wanted Judy to know of that hope and to realize who helped her. Later, when everything turned out as he planned, she would know. And he would have her.

Goodlove glanced away from the window at the men and horses and sleighs. Slattery's being inside did not bother him. The fact that Shaeffer and Wohl had failed to cut away enough of the bridge for the whole midsection to cave in grated on his mind. That was what happened when he allowed his underlings to handle an important job alone. Ketchuck had done his part by riding out from Yellowstone City last night with word that Slattery was borrowing Blumberg's sleigh. Goodlove had made one decision. He would handle the next try at Slattery himself. He would personally direct every step of setting him up . . .

He looked southward toward the wagon driven by Canby and Judy's Comanche. It was loaded with hay the two cowhands had cut down along the southern rim. Goodlove had sent them out early that morning to be certain they wouldn't be close when Slattery went into the river. The two of them, and Weaver, McPeck, and most of the Texans except Slattery, Murfee, and the Mexican, had forgotten how the trouble had started. Even Huffaker's woman had become friendlier. His men had built her shack and barn. He had personally given her and everyone else the right advice, and they trusted him. He owned half of the entire north end of the valley. The government had set up The Territorial Homestead Act to stop him or anyone else from being the original buyer of more than one homestead. But as long as the original owners failed to hold their hand and he could buy their acreage for pennies on the dollar, he eventually would own every inch of worthwhile range in Calligan Valley.

Gibson and the other dirt-eaters down along the southern rim could keep their one-horse spreads. Their sandy dry range did not interest Goodlove. He had talked the stubborn Texans into baling some of their hay for long storage, as he baled his hay. He had the barns filled with the hay and grain he would need once the Arctic blasts of winter set in. He was positive this winter would be a bad one. The blue sky would give way to more and more of the thick dark clouds that had sifted down over the Madisons and Gallatins in the last half hour. With the sun lowering toward the southwest peaks, the muck and slush of the ranch yard was already half frozen. All the weather had to do was run its course. He would have every cow he wanted. Every inch of land. And he would have Slattery's woman.

Jim Dancer watched the Comanche Indian and the cowboy circle their wagon wide around a snow drift. Dancer walked to Goodlove's side. He pointed into the mow, as though he talked of the hay and the men working inside the barn.

'Slattery'll be comin' out,' he said in a low voice. 'Jones and me could head toward the ranch and circle back 'round to the town bridge.'

Goodlove watched the workers. 'No. I don't want anything connected to us. You spread the word how Slattery and Murfee kept after you. Weaver and McPeck will talk with their neighbors. Everyone in the valley will know you were here, working.'

'What about Colburn? He was too close to the bridge. He might remember who he saw and he's got a big mouth.'

'He won't remember. He won't have time to remember.' He glanced to the north. During the few minutes they had talked the clouds had billowed up like gray fog to cover the white-tipped peaks. 'Snow will start soon.' He flicked a glance toward the house. 'We're going out tonight, and you'll get your chance.'

Dancer's lips cracked a smile. He liked this, the decision made and orders to follow. He began to start into the barn. 'I'll have Jones ready.'

'Don't say one word to Jones,' Goodlove snapped. 'To him or anyone else. I'll give the word. You do nothing unless I say so.'

'Sure. Sure, Mr. Goodlove.' Dancer stood with the long-pronged haying fork raised in his hands, not knowing what Goodlove would do or say next. After three years of working for the rancher, starting at the same time as Waco Jones when Goodlove hired them in Virginia City, he could never accurately guess what the man was thinking or planning.

Goodlove said, 'Finish in the barn. Keep clear of Slattery when he leaves. Weaver and McPeck have to see without any doubt that you're doing everything you can to keep from having trouble.'

Dancer nodded and eyed the house. The front door had opened. Slattery and Murfee

142

were coming outside. Goodlove said, 'Get working. That Wells woman will tell Miss Fiske exactly what happens. Later on, I don't want one person having reason to think we're here to do anything except help.'

CHAPTER FOURTEEN

The storm struck even sooner than Goodlove expected. Heavy black clouds covered the valley a quarter hour before Slattery and Murfee reached the bridge west of Yellowstone City. Slattery had wanted to stop at the Colburn ranch and spend some time with old John and his wife to help them remember the men they had seen weakening the bridge. But the cold wind and beginning snow made stopping impossible.

Augustin and the men he'd brought out from town with him had not been able to fight the rush of the water to drive new timbers into the riverbed. Instead they had thrown up wooden barriers at each end of the bridge so no one would try to cross. Slattery and Murfee crossed the Yellowstone City bridge while the snowy evening deepened into a frozen, windy twilight. Slattery felt his weakness now. His face was numb from the cold and the snow. His neck and shoulder throbbed with a slow pulsebeat that warned of his need for rest.

Four Corners was a cluster of dark shapes, the buildings of the town humped above the snowbanks. Yellowish lamplight streamed down from the windows and porches. The few people on the streets hunched against the weather, hurrying to get inside. Slattery and Murfee were entering Four Corners when the blizzard shut down around them. With it came a night as black and icy and suffocating as the frozen water of the river would have been, rushing and foaming below the broken bridge.

Blumberg waited on his porch. His small bony face and body were almost completely hidden in his bearskin hat and coat. He hurried down the steps of his store and into the street and climbed up onto the sleigh beside Slattery.

'I'll take her,' he yelled above the wail of the wind. 'There's coffee and food in the jail.'

'Thanks.' Slattery held onto the seat edge while he stepped down to the snow-covered walk. Beneath, the snow which had melted during the day, had frozen to sheer ice, and he had to move slowly and carefully so he wouldn't slip or fall.

In the office he sat for five minutes before he took off the sheepskin coat. His concern for Judy, his worry about her being crippled and about the way she thought and talked, and the long drives in the sleigh, had taken more out of him than he had realized. He was hungry and cold, his body like a dead weight. He stared at the hot potbelly stove. The high flame of the burning wood and the hot coffee felt good, giving him warmth he needed inside and outside his body.

He had to rest, one day, maybe two more days, before he could drive out to Colburn's. The chances of the old man and his wife remembering anything more than John had told him and Murfee already were slight. Yet it was all they had to go on, their only chance to in some way connect Ralph Goodlove, or the men who took his pay, to what had happened and what might happen in the future . . .

*   *   *

Goodlove had no idea of allowing Slattery or Murfee or anyone else to talk to John Colburn or his wife. Goodlove's main problem since the Texans had driven the Longhorns into the valley had been the river and its bridges. Calem Torrey had died because he had been seen trying to get away from one bridge after he had killed the big-mouthed pot-and-pan drummer. And the old man and his wife had almost been able to identify the men who had weakened the pilings of the second bridge.

Goodlove had made the men work faster so they finished storing the hay before the first flakes of snow started to fall. McPeck and Weaver had ridden off toward their houses. Goodlove and his men had left Canby and

145

Running Bear to close the barn, and then had headed westward with two of the sleighs.

As soon as they were out of sight, Goodlove had sent Dancer to check on the bridge repairs. Dancer returned with word that barriers had been built and no one could use the bridge. Goodlove allowed another half hour to pass to be certain Slattery and Murfee had more than enough time to reach Yellowstone City. Then he led his men across the bridge at the north end of the valley, bringing both of the sleighs with him, for he knew exactly what he intended to do.

He'd made no mistake about the coming winter. It would be worse than the freeze of '68. But he had made a mistake when he'd first built his ranch buildings on the Calligan's south bank. The range was too open there, not protected by the high bluffs of the valley's north end. The three-hundred head of Montana bred cattle he'd owned the past two years didn't trouble him. The Longhorns he'd bought were his worry. He'd made a point to separate the long yearling heifers which were facing their second winter. They were used to the open Texas range where snow was more powdery and seldom hid the grass beneath more than a few inches of unpacked cover. The young cattle hadn't learned the northern necessity of digging for their graze and many wouldn't know enough to go after the grass that lay under one or two feet of heavy, hardpacked snow. He'd talked the Texans into building larger barns and stocking ample feed. He hadn't done it for the homesteaders. The hay was for his own use. He'd need it once the long freeze set in. With twenty-five-hundred head in his herd, his existence depended on it.

The thought of the Colburn barn's mow and two of the old man's back stalls filled with hay was fresh in Goodlove's mind when he stopped the sleighs in front of the homesteader's darkened house. He handed the lines to Waco Jones and motioned to Dancer and Chino Neill to go into the barn. 'Load every bale in the stalls,' he ordered. 'Leave enough hay in the mow so it will look as though that's what caught fire. When you spread the oil, get it into every corner. Both buildings have to go up quick.'

'We will, Boss,' Dancer said.

'Damm it, don't call me Boss. Keep your voices down.'

Lamplight flickered on in the side bedroom. While Goodlove swung off into the snow, another lamp was lit in the front room. Goodlove drew a small double-barrelled Derringer from beneath his heavy buffalo-hide coat. He turned his head away from the wind and waited until Jones dismounted. Jones' tall body was bent forward, hazy in the dark and swirling howl of the storm, but Goodlove could see he had his sixgun in his hand.

'Don't wait to shoot,' Goodlove said. 'He

147

could answer the door with a gun or rifle.'

The lamplight brightened the shack's two front windows. Goodlove and Jones reached the door a fraction of a minute before it opened inward.

John Colburn squinted his eyes and stared out into the storm. He held the lamp in one hand. His other hand gripped his frayed blue bathrobe closed tight around his neck. His skinny wife, also holding her bathrobe closed tightly against the cold, waited behind him. Her bony face peered across her husband's shoulder to see who had awakened them.

'What? Oh, it's you, Mr. Goodlove!' the old man said. He turned his long, thin face toward his wife. 'It's all right, Sarah,' he began. 'They must've been lost—'

The words were cut off, silenced as Goodlove moved inside quickly. Colburn, shocked, thrown off balance, stumbled away from his wife so he wouldn't knock her down. He still held the lamp high when Jones' first bullet struck him.

Colburn was slammed back and died without another sound. His wife's face showed shock, then terror as three quick-fired bullets smashed her sideways against the wall. She was dead before she settled slowly to the wooden floor.

Goodlove grabbed the lamp from Colburn's hand. He raised it over his head and threw it through the open bedroom doorway where it exploded in a burst of flame against the wall.

'Empty the other lamps,' he told Jones. 'Get oil into every corner. I want every last piece of wood to burn.'

CHAPTER FIFTEEN

Barney Akkesson, his heavy cowhide coat covered with snow, rode into Yellowstone City the next morning with the news of the Colburn fire.

Akkesson was a lean, wide-shouldered cattlehand who had signed on with Slattery to help drive the Longhorns north from San Saba. He'd saved his wages to use as a down payment on his own homestead six miles north of the Colburn ranch. With the money he had borrowed from the Yellowstone City Bank, he had bought ten head of cattle, and it was because of six of his steers that he had been the one to find the ruins of the burned-out shack and barn.

'I seen they were gone when I got up this mornin',' he told Steve Murfee, 'so's I went huntin'. Both John and his missus are dead. Nothin' left of the barn or the house. I figured I'd better get right in and tell you.'

'So bad burned you couldn't even recognize them?' Murfee shook his head. 'Everything ruined? You didn't even find their cows?'

Akkesson's wind-chapped face moved from side to side. 'They must've drifted south like my beeves. That's what them Longhorns are doin'. Danged if I can make them stay where the updraft keeps the grass clear. Till they learn, I can't see how any of us'll keep them where they should be without huntin' them down and turnin' them after every storm.'

Slattery had pulled on his boots and a heavy sweater while the cowhand told what he had seen. His sheepskin coat had dried during the night. He buckled on his .44 Colt, and then buttoned the coat, thinking of talking to the old man yesterday, and of Sarah Colburn. He'd been too close to the old couple. All of the people who had come from Texas were close. It was sad, and it would be hard telling the others.

Slattery looked at Augustin Vierra. 'I'll go out with Steve and Barney and bring them in. Blumberg will let us use his sleigh.'

The Mexican nodded and took his sheepskin from the wall peg. He shook his head, not questioning Akkesson, but troubled. 'Both the house and the barn?' he said. He shook his head and looked at Slattery. 'There is one-hundred, maybe more, feet between the house and the barn. That is a wide space for flames to jump.' Icy wind and large wet snowflakes blew into the room when the deputy opened the door and stepped outside.

Slattery asked, 'They were both in the front

of the house, Barney? That's as far as they got?'

Nodding, the big rawboned homesteader said, 'They were lucky to get out of the bedroom. A small shack goes up so fast. Could've been their fireplace wasn't tight enough. We had good wood to build, but old John might not've built solid enough for this wind. I had a section of my roof start smoulderin' near the fireplace. I was lucky I caught it.'

Slattery finished buttoning his coat. He pulled his hat down tight and took a Winchester carbine from the rack. Murfee watched Slattery for a moment and chose a Spencer rifle.

'You sure you're able to go?' Murfee questioned. 'You were worn out last night.'

'I'm able.' Slattery checked the carbine's load. He had felt woozy when he'd dressed at midmorning and had stood at the ice-sheathed window and watched Myron Blumberg's plow fight a losing battle at keeping the intersection clear. Even the worse Texas storms were nothing like this. He went to the window and rubbed the steam from the glass. The snow and wind that had lessened at midmorning had added barely an inch of depth since then, yet he knew it would close in before dark. The intense quiet of Four Corners, the drifts four to five feet deep on the south side, accented the silken gray overcast which would hang on

151

until the north wind whipped down again from the divide.

*   *   *

Akkesson tied his horse to the tailgate of the sleigh and climbed up onto the seat with Slattery and Murfee. Blumberg's bay mare had little trouble moving across the wind-packed snow. They were a quarter-mile beyond the river bridge when a yell from behind made Murfee pull back on the reins.

Donald Ketchuck from the land office had followed them out of town. The tall government agent, red-faced and shivering despite his thick bearskin-lined coat and two pairs of trousers, spurred his mount to make it run through the deep drifts.

'Vierra told me about the Colburns,' he called before he reached the sleigh. His eyes switched from Slattery to Murfee. 'I had to go to the jail to find out why you were leaving. I should have been informed.'

'Not much you c'n do,' said Murfee, shaking the lines. 'All's we're doin' is lookin' and takin' them back for burial.'

'I should have been informed. Anything that has to do with the land comes under my jurisdiction. I have to decide what to do.'

'Why?' Slattery asked.

The land agent's annoyance had calmed. 'Government land that has been homesteaded can be sold again if there are no family claims. The Colburns didn't have children. You, or anyone who is interested in buying that property, can put in bids.'

'I'm not interested.' He looked at Murfee and Akkesson. 'None of us is interested.'

Ketchuck nodded, his voice calmer and official. 'Well, I'm responsible and have to report this to my superiors. I don't enjoy something like this happening any more than you people. But it is part of my responsibility.'

The land agent stopped talking and continued to ride alongside the three men. He sat hunched over, using the sleigh to break the force of the wind and falling snow.

Slattery watched Ketchuck. The irritation he felt toward the man would not leave him. The small amount of business he had done in Ketchuck's office hadn't given him a chance to know the agent, but now he wondered about him. Ketchuck could have waited until the dead man and his wife were brought in. Yet, he hadn't. Ketchuck kept his mouth bitten into a thin line, but it wasn't simply because of the cold . . . sorrow, for the Colburn couple, a deep feeling about such a terrible tragedy . . . Slattery wasn't sure. He was certain that what Barney Akkesson said about the Longhorns was true. They passed eight cows in the next half hour, each animal drifting southward with its rump to the weather. Along the river's edge, the bluish line of the stream showed more and more of the thick glaze of ice. He could see the dark blots of cattle off toward Mal Weaver's homestead. Every cow would have to bc turned back out of the deeper snow, the solid drifts of white that stretched southward toward the stark cliffs and peaks of granite rearing straight up into the lead-gray sky.

Akkesson, who had bought his land north of the river, had been one of the few Texans who could face a winter of deep freeze. Even the few areas of grass that had been swept clear by the wind yesterday had a two or three inch cover of snow today. Each new storm would add more depth. Eventually, the southern pass would be buried under twenty or twenty-five feet of the packed, frozen whiteness. Only at the northern end of the valley would the steady updraft from the bottomlands have a chance of keeping the grass clear to any extent. The timberline of the upper Calligan, heavy stands of box elder and ash and conifers, gave a natural protection to stock. The stream would never completely ice over because the rush of water down from the mountains wouldn't let it. Slattery studied the river and the flat to the north. He sat with the other men in silence while the sleigh approached the blackened skeleton beams of what had been the Colburn home.

'Ketchuck and Barney will take care of Old John and Sarah,' Steve Murfee said, breaking into Slattery's thoughts. The lawman handed Slattery the reins and leaned across the seatboard to take the tarpaulins he had brought from Blumberg's store. As Slattery slowed, then stopped the sleigh, Murfee stood. 'I'll lower the tailgate.'

Snow covered most of the ruins. Only the stone chimney and fireplace and the charred two-by-four framing showed where the house had been. The barn was completely burned except for the front peak of the roof. That and part of the mow had caved in. The few half-destroyed boards that remained jutted above a three-foot drift like black, broken fenceposts.

Slattery stepped down and walked to where Akkesson and the land agent cleared the snow from the bodies of the old man and woman. Both were badly burned. Akkesson straightened and looked toward Murfee near the ruins of the barn.

'Give us a hand, Steve,' he called.

Murfee did not answer. He kicked snow away from the charred wood of a back stall. He crouched down and swept more snow clear with his gloves. He glanced across his shoulder. 'Tom, Barney, look at this.' His long, hard-boned face was troubled. He gave his attention to the stall's earth floor while he kicked harder at the snow to clear more of it away.

Slattery reached Murfee ahead of Akkesson. 'What's the matter?'

Murfee had the stall almost empty of snow. The ground was frozen solid, the white that was left black in spots with the remains of burned hay.

'I was out here when Colburn's hay was stored,' he said. 'John had some of the hay baled with wire and piled in these two back stalls.' He kept clearing the last traces of the snow away. 'It was baled with wire. I don't see no wire layin' around.'

'Yes,' Akkesson said. 'John hired Jackie Pruitt and the Mercer kid to help with the baling, and up in the mow. I saw them out here workin'.'

Murfee pulled the remains of a stallboard loose and dug at the snow in the next stall. 'There'd be plenty ashes from bales of hay,' he said. 'And every last bit of hay wouldn't burn, not once the roof gave in and the wind started them drifts.' He swept the snow away harder. Akkesson used another board as a shovel. Together he and Murfee uncovered the floor of both rear stalls.

Murfee was sweating when he straightened. 'Not one trace of hay,' he said. 'John's cows couldn't've finished what the old man had baled.'

'Damn right,' Akkesson added. 'He was stocked for all winter. Only thing I can figure is he might've sold some.'

'He could have done just that,' Ketchuck said. The land agent had managed to move the

156

two tarpaulin-covered bodies into the wagon bed. He had driven the sleigh across the yard and stopped near the men. 'John was in my office a week ago with enough money to pay off the entire loan on his land.'

Murfee said, 'He say who offered to buy his hay?'

Ketchuck was thoughtful. He glanced at the canvas that held the dead man and woman. 'I believe he said Weaver offered to buy some.'

'And Goodlove,' Barney Akkesson said. 'He's kept his hired hands busy fillin' both Ian Huffaker's woman's barn and Judy Fiske's. His man Neill was over to my place askin' if I'd sell or lease part of my graze.'

'We'll check that.' Murfee threw the board on top of the drift. 'Now, Tom.'

Slattery nodded and turned with Murfee.

Ketchuck said, 'Wouldn't it be better if we rested?' He stared up into the heavy gray clouds, holding one gloved hand over his eyes to ward off the sparse fall of snowflakes. 'It's so late, we wouldn't get to Goodlove's until dark. It would be eight or nine o'clock before we reached Weaver's.'

'That's right. It'll be late,' Murfee said. He paused at the sleigh's step plate until Akkesson and Slattery climbed onto the seat ahead of him. Then he pulled himself up alongside Slattery. Ketchuck had not moved. The land agent stood flat-footed in the snow, watching them.

'I don't like the looks of the weather,' Ketchuck warned. 'I don't think—'

'I don't care what you think.' Murfee gripped the reins and pulled with his left hand to swing the sleigh. 'You got a responsibility in this. You said so yourself. Mount up and follow us.'

CHAPTER SIXTEEN

Ketchuck wanted to turn his horse and run. He had ridden out with the acting sheriff and Slattery because he knew Ralph Goodlove would want to know exactly what happened at the Colburn place. But he hadn't believed it possible that he would be heading for Goodlove's ranch. The afternoon was so cold the icy freeze penetrated his coat's thickness and slowed his circulation. He expected the storm would start again. The wind blew too hard, raw and biting and whipping the drifting snow into his face. He kept hoping the storm would strike, despite his cold and discomfort. Yet in the hour and a half the horses and sleigh took to reach the northern bridge across the Calligan, the clouds only became heavier and blacker and uglier without the steady fall of snowflakes becoming thicker.

Now, while they crossed the bridge, Ketchuck scanned the dark growth of timber

158

and the giant granite walls and cliffs that rose almost vertically above them. The white-covered mountains seemed to crowd in on him, to move toward him as though they might tumble over and bury the sleigh, horses, and men. That was funny, terrifyingly funny, Ketchuck thought, for his world could tumble over and he would be ruined after they reached Goodlove's ranch. He hadn't wanted anything like this to happen. He hadn't wanted the two men from Texas, Huffaker and McDonald, to be hunted and shot the way they were. Or to have that poor pot-and-pan drummer murdered so brutally.

The plans he had made with Goodlove in Helena were so simple. He would handle the legal end and see to it the land rights Goodlove could acquire were not questioned in the Washington Bureau. Goodlove was to apply pressure to the homesteaders and buy out each settler who failed. He was to stay within the law, and he had, until the two Texans came a month ago. Ketchuck glanced at the wagon bed, thinking of the pitiful old man and woman lying under the tarpaulins. There had been absolutely no need for harming them . . . Goodlove had gone too far, had done too much, and Ketchuck had no idea what might happen now.

Slattery sat straight and stiff on the wagon seat. He had barely spoken a word, but he showed his thoughts and feelings by pumping his carbine at ten minute intervals to make sure the snow and cold didn't affect its action. Slattery and Murfee were on the right track and they knew it. Ketchuck watched the two men. He slowed his mount and hung back behind the sleigh, his fear building more and more with every step the horses took.

The road leading to Goodlove's Circle G showed no signs that anyone had left or ridden into the ranch since the storm began. Ketchuck had not understood Goodlove's idea of working with the settlers and helping them store grain and hay. Now, looking at the snow drifted high over the grass, he did understand the value of Goodlove's having lived eight winters in this mountain country.

The wind-blown columns of smoke rose ahead, one from the sprawling two-story house with a large veranda that stretched across the entire front, the other from the log bunkhouse a hundred yards to its left.

Ketchuck relaxed a bit and breathed easier. Goodlove had only to act friendly and show he was shocked and disgusted at what had been done to the elderly couple. Ketchuck lost his hope that would happen when the front door opened and Goodlove stepped into view. The big cattleman wore his winter coat, but it was unbuttoned in the front, showing his holstered sixgun.

Goodlove held one hand above his eyes and stared through the falling snow to watch the men in the sleigh and the land agent approach his home. Ketchuck raised his arm and waved to him. Goodlove did not move. The bunkhouse door opened. Dancer, Jones, and four more of Goodlove's hired hands stepped outside. Each man carried a rifle or a carbine. They reached the porch before Murfee stopped the sleigh in the wide yard between the buildings, and they stood together waiting for Goodlove's orders.

Goodlove moved to the edge of the porch. His hard, controlled expression did not change. 'What do you want, Sheriff?'

Murfee swung down from the seat and walked to the tailgate. While he pulled the tarpaulins off the bodies of Colburn and his wife, a heavy silence, a taut quiet broken only by the wind, spread over the yard.

'This was done last night,' Murfee said. He stood with his right leg clear of the sleigh, his coat unbuttoned. 'Whoever did it took Colburn's hay with them. Every last bale he had in his barn.'

Goodlove muttered a curse. 'That's it then.' He nodded to his cowhands. 'Relax. You can go back inside if you want.'

Not one of the line of men moved to leave.

Goodlove's face turned from his men to Murfee. 'I thought you were coming out because of last night.' He gestured at his own barn. The high double doors were closed. A path had been dug to the left door, but the

161

storm had drifted it almost completely over again. 'Someone came up behind my barn and tried to get into my mow, Sheriff. Jones heard them and went out to look. He got a shot off and I figured he might've hit him.'

'I did hit him,' Jones said. 'One of them, anyway. We found sleigh tracks but they're all covered now.'

Slattery said. 'And you let them get away because of the storm?'

'The storm didn't stop anything,' Goodlove told him. 'You see only six of my hands. I have fourteen riders. The rest of them are either out hazing back my beeves that have drifted off my land or they're hunting for that sleigh.' He stared at the charred bodies, his manner cold and deliberate. 'That's what happened to John and Sarah. If Jonesie didn't wake up, I don't know what could've happened here.'

'You've got fourteen men,' Slattery said flatly. 'Take some man to try something against those odds.'

'That's right, it does. And I can handle them. I won't need your help, Sheriff. You drove out all this distance for nothing.'

Slattery looked at Murfee, who said, 'Your mow's filled then?'

'Right to the top. I've given orders to gun anyone who tries taking one bale of hay.' He nodded from the lawman to Akkesson. 'I tried helping his kind. Weaver, McPeck, all of them. But from here on, we shoot, Sheriff. I need every bit of feed I've got. One of the homesteaders did that. You better find him before I do.'

Akkesson said, 'Look here, Mr. Goodlove. I don't accuse you.'

'You're damn right you don't. You don't stay on my land, Mister. You don't let your cows drift onto my land.' He shook his head and again stared disgustedly at the sleigh. 'I tried with you people. Anything I have to do with you from now on is strictly business. That goes for you. It goes for that Weaver too.'

'Weaver?' said Murfee. 'Why Weaver?'

Goodlove's mouth cracked a smile. 'He's got himself a sleigh, Sheriff. You know he converted that Mex wagon of his. Now, if you're satisfied I didn't put those people in that wagon, you go ask your questions to some of Slattery's Texans.'

'Mr. Goodlove,' Ketchuck said. 'It's freezing cold. We've been out most of the day.'

'You can stay out the rest of the day. And the night. You knew what the sheriff was thinking when he headed out here.' He eyed the sleigh and added, 'Sheriff, I don't want you on my land. Not without damn good reason.'

Murfee didn't answer.

Ketchuck had retreated to his horse. Clumsily, in his bulky clothing, he hauled himself into his saddle. 'Sheriff?' he said, glancing at the sky. 'I didn't want this, Sheriff. If we're going to Weaver's, we"ll have to

163

hurry.'

Murfee turned to Akkesson. 'Go back to your place, Barney.' And to Slattery, 'It'll be a long ride back.'

Slattery studied Goodlove. While the land agent had spoken, he had seen something new in the rancher's expression, something that could be irritation, or it could be a knowing confidence. He tried to keep the recognition from showing in his voice. 'You want to warm up, Mr. Ketchuck,' he said, 'we'll stop off at Fiske's. And at Weaver's too, if the storm gets bad enough.'

'Fine. Fine.' Ketchuck looked away from Goodlove while he turned his mount.

Goodlove watched Slattery and Murfee climb onto the sleigh's seat. Akkesson had untied his horse, and as soon as Murfee swung the sleigh, he mounted and rode alongside the wagon seat. Dancer started onto the steps as soon as he was certain the riders and men on the sleigh were beyond earshot.

'Slattery's wise to Ketchuck,' he said. 'Give him time, he'll work on him.'

Goodlove spit onto the snow. Dancer fingered the stock of his Enfield rifle, watching. He knew the rancher had seen how Slattery had studied each man, how Slattery had watched the land agent's nervousness. Ketchuck had given Slattery an opening to work on. The rancher had seen that as clearly as the other men.

'I didn't mean Ketchuck'll give anythin' away, Boss,' Dancer offered. 'But Slattery can do some checkin' in Helena.'

Frowning, Goodlove looked once more toward the hazy shadows of the sleigh, the horses and riders. Akkesson had left the others to head for his own shack. Akkesson wouldn't be a problem. Goodlove drew his solid gold stem-winder from his vest pocket. Three-sixteen. The porch thermometer stood at ten below zero. It would drop to twenty-five below before midnight. By six or seven, the wind would increase in its bite, driving a streaming mass of snow down from the north, making a real ground blizzard, exactly what he needed.

'You men eat,' he said. 'Chino and LeBlanc, rig up the sleighs. If they're planning to stop at Fiske's, they won't reach Weaver's until about six.'

'We're hittin' them,' Dancer said.

Goodlove nodded. 'At Weaver's. We'll load his hay and leave them like the Colburn's. Every one of them.'

Waco Jones shifted his stance from his left foot to his right. 'Mr. Goodlove, there's a little girl at Weaver's.'

Goodlove's voice snapped like the wind. 'Slattery will be there. And that two-bit deputy who thinks he's a lawman. I said everybody.' A small flake of snow touched his cheek. He raised one hand and brushed away the wetness. Then he smiled up at the falling

165

flakes. 'We'll have better cover than last night. Eat, and be ready in a half hour.'

CHAPTER SEVENTEEN

'Slow down,' Slattery said to Steve Murfee. He glanced across his shoulder at Ketchuck who had fallen behind the sleigh. The land agent was hunched over in the saddle, his head lowered out of the wind and heavy snowfall.

'Ketchuck! Don't hold us back, Ketchuck!' Slattery called. He leaned his body toward the rider and called again.

The sleigh slowed and Ketchuck's horse broke through a deep drift and came closer. The land agent's face was red from the cold. Snow had caked along his eyebrows into the wrinkles of his eyes and cheeks and mouth.

'Go ahead of us,' Slattery told him. 'Ask Lute Canby if he'll have a horse ready for us. Blumberg's is about worn out.'

'No, I'll stay with you. I c'n stay.'

'Ride ahead. You'll have a chance to warm up till we get there.'

'Lottie'll make coffee,' Murfee said. 'Tell her to. We'll be right behind you.'

Ketchuck tried to shake his head but he was so cold and rigid he didn't succeed. 'Ride ahead,' Slattery repeated. 'We'll need the horse so we can start right away. We've got to get back to town before the storm really hits.'

Ketchuck rode past the sleigh without offering further argument. Blumberg's mare walked slowly, careful of the hard-crusted surface, slowing even more as each drift had to be bypassed or crossed. Within two minutes the land agent had vanished into the hazy grayness, the late afternoon made darker by the swirling snow. Murfee said, 'He's coverin' something. You saw him back there.'

'We'll check his books when we get in. Tonight, so he doesn't have a chance to make changes.'

'Tom, that's government property.'

'You're sheriff. He won't refuse you asking. Ketchuck or anyone else isn't getting out of this valley till spring. We'll have time.'

Murfee nodded and tightened his grip on the reins. Far ahead a stream of lamplight showed through the dusk and snow. Ketchuck and his horse were a momentary blur before the haze closed in again. Slattery was cold to the bone, despite the heaviness of his sheepskin. His mouth was dry, his lips and skin chapped and raw, yet he felt strong and even hopeful.

Steve had also seen what had passed between Goodlove and Ketchuck. Slattery didn't know what it meant, wasn't positive it would lead to anything, but it was the first real opening they had. Just by making a point of checking the books, he might worry the land agent enough to go to Goodlove for help. It could be the first step toward learning something . . .

The snow-covered shapes of the barn and house came into view. Shadowy forms of men moved about in the yard. Slattery squinted against the icy flakes, straining his eyes to see who the men were.

Both Lute Canby and Running Bear had crossed the yard to meet Ketchuck. They spoke together for a few moments, then the land agent dismounted and went up the porch steps and into the house. Running Bear, looking tall and husky bundled in his sheepskin, took hold of the land agent's bridle to lead the horse into the barn. Canby waited in the middle of the yard. The stubby old cattleman stood with both of his gloved hands protecting his face. He shouted to Slattery and Murfee before the lawman drew the mare to a halt.

'There's hot coffee inside, but Judy and Lottie ain't here,' he told them. 'They went to the Weavers' early this afternoon, before the storm set in again. I figure they'll stay there the night.'

'They went out?' Slattery said. 'You realized it would get worse.'

Canby shook his head. 'You know Judy. She's been locked in so long she had to get out. She's been to the Weavers' before, and she and Lottie have stayed over with them.'

Murfee said, 'Lottie should've had more brains.' He glanced at the barn doors. Running Bear had left one side open wide enough to have them see he was leading Judy's brown team horse from its stall. 'We'll hitch up for you,' the Indian horsebreaker called. 'You want to get coffee, I'll stay outside.'

'We'll change horses and leave right away.' Slattery stared at Canby. 'Lute, how about Ketchuck bunkin' with you till the weather clears?'

'Sure. We've got plenty room.'

'Good. He can use some rest.' He looked toward the house while Murfee drove the sleigh in past the open barn door. 'Lute, go tell Ketchuck he can stay and we'll send the sleigh out for him in the morning.'

*   *   *

Ketchuck quickly set down the steaming coffee mug he had held in both hands because of his stiffened fingers. 'No, I can't stay,' he said to Canby. 'I've got to get back to town.'

'We've got room,' the cowhand told him. 'You won't be puttin' anyone out with Judy and Lottie spendin' the night with the Weavers.'

'No. No, thanks.' He tried to pull his icy, frozen leather gloves onto his hands. His fingers were so cold and rigid they wouldn't do what he wanted, and he let out a low,

169

exasperated moan. Goodlove could have allowed him to get warm. He realized the rancher had to act out his part, but he could have at least allowed him to spend a few minutes near a stove. He was so cold, frozen, his face and ears smarting and beginning to itch from the heat. He wanted to stay inside this warm house, to become warm and eat and rest and sleep. But he didn't dare let Slattery and Murfee continue on without him. They suspected he had some connection to Goodlove. He had seen that in their faces. Goodlove had seen it. But they weren't certain of anything yet. Neither of them was certain, so they would start asking questions and looking around, and they might want to spend time searching through his records in his office.

Ketchuck followed Canby to the front door. The snow seemed thicker. The sky was darker. Slattery and Murfee worked with the Comanche cattlehand inside the barn changing the sleigh horses. Ketchuck hurried back to the table and gripped the steaming mug with both gloved hands. The hot liquid felt good going down. Every second he could stay out of the weather was valuable, precious to him. He poured another mugful. He sipped the burning hot coffee, trying to relax.

Boots thumped on the porch. Running Bear opened the door and looked into the kitchen. 'Slattery and Murfee said they'll have the sleigh out here first thing in the morning if you want to stay.'

Quickly Ketchuck gulped down the last hot mouthful. He hurried outside, his body hunched over as a defense against the freezing sting. The sleigh had already moved from the yard. Ketchuck straightened then, forgetting the snow and wind and cold while he ran into the barn to mount and follow before Murfee and Slattery got too far ahead.

*　　　*　　　*

Slattery was the first one to see the sleigh appear in front of them. He knew they had passed the Huffaker house though no lights could be seen through the dark and the storm. Ketchuck, not saying a word, rode behind their sleigh. They were a quarter mile from Mal Weaver's ranch when the barely discernable shape of a horse loomed up ahead. Then the sleigh drawn by the horse, with three people on the driver's seat, materialized out of the gloom.

Slattery reached for the Winchester. He pumped the weapon as Murfee swung the stallion to the right.

'Hey, Tom! Steve!' Mal Weaver's voice shouted to them. 'Hey, you two!' He looked as if he was packed in tight on the seat by his cowhide coat and hat and the blankets that covered his legs and thighs and all but the faces of the two who rode with him.

Murfee drew in alongside the carreta, the high-built wagon rocking on its thick, home-forged iron runners. The two passengers were Judy Fiske and Lottie Wells. Both women wore hooded bearskin capes and heavy coats, both hunched down close together, their heads bent to keep their eyes free of snow.

'What are you doin' out here?' Murfee questioned angrily.

Lottie said, 'We're goin' home. Can't you see that?'

Murfee shook his head. 'You'll catch your death goin' three more miles against this wind. Mal, you should know better.'

'We asked them to stay overnight,' Mal explained. 'But they wanted to go home. We couldn't talk them into stayin'.'

'Steve's right,' Slattery told them. 'You'll be another hour in this weather. Swing around, Mal.'

Judy said, 'There isn't enough room at the Weavers'.' Only her lips moved. Weaver and Lottie had placed her so she was huddled between them, giving her the most protection from the weather. 'We can reach home all right.'

'Turn back,' Slattery again told the rancher. He saw Judy's expression, her lips bitten tight and her eyes flashing. She said nothing while Weaver swung the carreta sleigh southward.

Murfee held Blumberg's sleigh close behind

the women to break the force of the wind. The snow thickened more in the half-hour it took to push through the deepening drifts. When the drivers halted their horses at Weaver's doorstep, Slattery and Murfee climbed off to help the women. Ketchuck headed his horse straight for the barn.

Slattery reached up to lift Judy. Her mouth was still as tight and angry, her manner aloof. 'Mal will carry me,' she said. 'You're not strong enough yet.'

Slattery didn't answer. He slipped one arm around her shoulders, and with the other hand he wrapped the blanket tight around her legs. 'Easy now,' he said. 'Bend forward.'

'I can't bend. You know that. You're not strong enough.'

'You're wrong, both times,' Slattery said, lifting her. His neck throbbed, a slow pulse that quickened once he held her. But he felt no pain. He moved onto the bottom step.

The front door opened. Nancy Weaver and her daughter crowded the doorway to look outside. Six-year-old Linda called to her father.

'Judy and Lottie are stayin' with us,' Weaver told his family. 'Let them get in while I handle the horses. Help them, Nancy.'

'Oh, Mommy! Mommy!' Linda said. 'They're going to stay. We can make popcorn!' Her blond curly hair shook while she jumped up and down. 'Can we, Mommy?'

173

'Of course,' her mother said. Smiling happily, the woman and her little girl backed from the doorway so Slattery could carry Judy Fiske inside.

CHAPTER EIGHTEEN

Ralph Goodlove leaned forward on the seat of his sleigh and took his Winchester carbine from beneath the blanket he had wrapped around the weapon. He'd sat on the lever and chamber during the two-hour ride from his ranch. Despite the cover of the blanket and his body, the iron was cold, and he pumped the lever to loosen the action. The blizzard was a continuous high scream of wind. Weaver's barn, two-hundred feet away, was almost completely closed off from his view. Dancer had ridden ahead to get a look into the barn ten minutes ago, time enough for him to learn whether Slattery and Murfee had reached the homesteader's house.

Goodlove pulled back on the reins to stop his two horses. He could see the figure of a man, bent over against the wind to stay erect, moving through the yard toward him. He yanked on the rope he'd strung between the two sleighs to keep them together. Jones, driving the second large wagon, stopped his horses alongside the lead sleigh.

174

Dancer took another two minutes to reach them. He climbed up onto the step plates between the sleighs. 'They're in the house,' he told them, his words barely audible under the screech and wail of the storm. 'Blumberg's sleigh's in the barn. Weaver's too.'

'Ketchuck with them?' Goodlove bent over close to the gunman. 'You're sure?'

'His horse is in one of the back stalls. Some of the hay was moved out of the stalls to make room for the extra horses. One of them will have to come out to hitch up to the sleigh. Unless they're staying all night.'

Chino Neill, on the seat beside Jones, pounded his arms across his chest. 'They're gonna stay, we better get inside quick. Another hour and we'll freeze out here.'

Dancer said, 'We could move the big wagon 'round behind the barn and start takin' the hay. We'd have most of it loaded 'fore we fired the house.'

'We're not taking the hay until we finish them inside,' Goodlove told him. 'We'll leave more hay than we did at Colburn's. I don't want anyone to have questions.'

'You're gonna need all the feed we can get, once the freeze sets in.'

'We'll leave more of the hay.' Goodlove motioned to Jones. 'We'll drive both wagons around behind the barn. That will get the horses out of the storm and give them a breather. We'll wait inside. Dancer, you'll watch from the door. We'll be ready when one of them comes out to hitch up.'

'I c'n cut him down in the yard.'

'No, two of them might come out. Weaver might come with Slattery and Murfee, and we can finish all of them at once. Then you and Waco will go into the house for the woman and girl.'

Dancer nodded and Jones started his sleigh toward the barn. Goodlove slid the Winchester under the blanket and sat on the weapon while he moved his horses ahead.

He knew they would have to hit within an hour. The temperature was falling too fast. At forty or fifty below, animals died quickly, their lungs froze. He'd even seen trees explode like a rifle shot at those temperatures. He could lose cattle tonight. He would have to be out before daybreak with his men to force every head that drifted too far south back toward the river. The sand and water in the shallows would be frozen thick enough to drive the herd across to the north side. He'd lose every last steer if he didn't get them out of the open range and up into the timber . . . Once Weaver was taken care of, Akkesson would be next. He'd have the entire north range as his own. Nothing could hold him back after he left Slattery and Murfee dead out here tonight.

Slattery swallowed a mouthful of coffee and watched Judy who half-lay, half-sat in the large chair that had been moved into the kitchen from the living room. Nancy Weaver had warmed over some beef stew for him, Murfee, and Ketchuck. Slattery had tried to carry on a conversation with Judy, but she had remained quiet while they had eaten. Ketchuck sat beside the stove trying to get as much warmth as possible into his body before they left. Murfee had gulped down his food. Now he played a game of checkers against the combined team of Lottie Wells and Linda Weaver. The little girl giggled, then laughed happily. 'We've got you! We've got you two kings to one!'

'I'm not done yet,' Murfee told them. 'I'll show you.'

Judy's head was turned toward the fireplace, her eyes watching the three checker players. Her face was lined and tired. Slattery stood and walked to her. She looked up at him.

'They know how to be so happy,' she said. 'Children.'

Slattery grinned. 'Steve's as big a kid as she is.' The grin held and he motioned to the coffee. 'You sure you don't want some? It's good and hot.'

'No, I don't care for any.'

Slattery nodded. Being inside for longer than an hour had given him the rest and strength he needed. The horses had been rubbed and grained by Weaver. They would be able to complete the trip back to town. The main problem which bothered him was Judy's

177

silence, her almost reluctance to speak of anything with him. She had continually watched Lottie and Steve and the child, yet she didn't even seem to be part of the group. It was as though she'd separated herself from them and wanted to keep it that way.

Slattery said, 'Mal says he'll be glad to have you and Lottie stay till the storm's over. You both can help—'

'I can't help,' she interrupted. 'I want to go home where I won't be a bother.'

'Judy, you're not bothering anybody. Don't let this lick you. Mal and Nancy are glad you're here. Look how happy Linda is.'

'I told you, Tom.' She would not meet his eyes. The game had ended and Linda was shouting, 'We won! We won! We beat you!' Lottie and Murfee laughed with the child. Nancy Weaver held out a dishcloth to her daughter. 'Now that you've won, help me win with these.'

'Oh, Mommy. I want to play with Steve and Miss Lottie.'

Murfee pushed his chair back and straightened. 'We've got to get movin',' he told the little girl. 'You help Lottie and your mother.'

Linda stood beside her chair. She looked at Steve and Lottie. 'If you're going to get married,' she questioned, 'why doesn't Miss Lottie go with you? My mommy always goes with Daddy.'

178

Murfee lifted his sheepskin from the back of the chair. 'Miss Lottie will be coming with me, pretty soon,' he said. He circled one arm around Lottie's shoulders. 'She'll be with me soon enough.' He dropped his arm and said to Ketchuck while he slid his right hand into the coatsleeve, 'Come on. There's a long drive ahead.'

Lottie held Slattery's sheepskin open for him to put on. Judy said, 'Lottie, you and Steve don't have to hold up your plans. The weather will clear in one or two days. Don't put off your wedding because of me.'

Lottie smiled from Judy to Slattery, then at Murfee and Weaver who were buttoning their heavy coats. 'We don't mind waiting. I want a house in town we can move into. If Steve's going to stay on as sheriff, I won't live outside Yellowstone City.'

'You shouldn't wait,' Judy said. 'I wish—' She didn't finish the sentence, but went on quickly, 'Get all the happiness you can. I'm all right without you, Lottie. Go in tonight if you want.'

'I'll wait,' said Lottie.

'Don't just because of me. I haven't asked you to.' Judy's words were brisk, as sharp and cold as the rush of air that blew in when Weaver opened the kitchen's rear door. Lottie didn't answer. She walked to the small back entry with Murfee. Ketchuck had taken his time dressing. He pulled on his gloves and

179

followed the other men. Nancy Weaver raised the kitchen window shade so she could watch the men leave.

Slattery stared directly into Judy's face. 'You shouldn't talk to Lottie like that,' he said. 'She's done all she can to help.'

'I don't want people pitying me.'

Slattery's tone softened. 'Judy, there's a good chance you'll walk again. You haven't even tried to get on your feet. I've told you it doesn't matter. We can still do what we've planned.'

'We can't still do anything.' Judy shook her head back and forth emphatically. 'You know how I feel about your being burdened with me.' Her lips thinned, the line of her jaw tightened. 'The person who made me like this wants me. He deserves what he gets. Exactly what he gets.'

'Tom,' Murfee called as he opened the door. 'The glass has dropped five degrees. We'd better get movin'.'

Slattery stared at Judy for another few seconds, but she would not meet his eyes. 'I'll come for a visit as soon as I can,' he said. He took his Winchester and followed Murfee outside.

The wail and scream of the wind smothered the crack of a rifle fired from near the storm-blurred haziness of the barn. Ketchuck sprawled flat. Murfee threw himself sideways into a snowbank, but Weaver panicked and tried to run, stumbling through the drifts toward his house.

Another rifle banged as Slattery, in a single motion, reached out to grab Weaver and drop to the cover of the snow. His fingers barely gripped Weaver's pants leg before the bullet zipped by inches above his head. Weaver broke away and continued his plodding dash, making himself a clear target in the stream of lamplight slanting down from the kitchen window.

'Down! Mal, get down!' Slattery yelled. And while the terrified Weaver quickened his stride, Slattery screamed toward the house, 'Douse the lamp! Put it out so we can't be seen!'

CHAPTER NINETEEN

Weaver scrambled onto the steps, his arms and the fingers of his hands outstretched to catch hold of the doorknob. One rifle, then a second slammed at the same instant from the barn. Weaver fell forward, sprawled out over the stoop. The door was yanked open and Nancy Weaver suddenly was silhouetted in the doorway as she bent down to try to help her husband into the kitchen.

Slattery and Murfee both had fired at the men who'd hit Weaver. Nancy's voice

181

screamed into the yard, her high-pitched, terrified words carried on the wind, blending with the blasts of gunfire.

'Help me! Help! Lottie! Judy! Help me!'

Two weapons banged from behind the half-opened barn door. Two more shots came from the barn's left side. Bullets exploded snow into Slattery's face while he fired a second time, a third. He could see Murfee pumping his Spencer rifle. He had crawled toward where Ketchuck lay flat on his stomach digging with both hands to burrow into the depth of a high drift.

'Use the snow!' Slattery shouted. 'Steve, dig for cover!'

He triggered off another bullet, rolled to the left, pumping the weapon to lever another cartridge into the chamber. Three, four, maybe five of them, he kept thinking. Two behind the doors, the others using the barn's corner for cover. Bullets zipped, zinged above his head, burned through the snow as he fired, pumped, squeezed the trigger again. Men's voices called to each other near the barn. Their words were indistinguishable to Slattery, lost under the wail and roar of the wind.

Slattery glanced around while he rolled into the deeper snow. Lottie was alongside Nancy, the two women straining to drag Weaver inside. Beyond them, clearly visible in the lamplight, Judy had pushed herself to her feet, her body bent over the table, her arms

182

outstretched, holding the table top so she wouldn't fall . . .

*   *   *

Behind the barn door, Goodlove snapped wildly at Dancer lying prone near him. 'Get ready to go out to the side of the barn. I'll cover you.'

'We've got cover.' Dancer hugged the earth, keeping his body as low as possible. 'We should stay.'

'No, they can corner us! Get out with Waco and Neill!'

Staring into the storm, he crouched lower and shot into the snow where he had last seen Murfee. Murfee did not return the shot. Goodlove swung his carbine and put his next bullet into the drift where he judged Slattery would be . . . He'd been right to send Jones and Chino Neill out to circle around back and down the left side of the barn and wait at the building's corner. They had Slattery spotted and centered their fire on him.

Goodlove raised his carbine. One bullet would block the open doorway with Weaver and one of the women. As they struggled to get Weaver inside, the lamplight streaming from the window and onto the stoop made them perfect targets. He didn't squeeze the trigger. He could see Judy Fiske was in the kitchen! She was standing up staring outside

183

. . . He'd had no idea she was in Weaver's home. He'd thought . . . it didn't matter what he'd thought. He'd wanted Judy Fiske, injured, crippled or not, but he couldn't leave a witness, no man or woman or child.

He'd waited too long. The women gave Weaver a final tug, dragging him in past the door frame, and the door was slammed shut blacking out the wide square of lamplight. Just as quickly, the kitchen shade was pulled down.

'Go, Dancer!' he shouted, triggering off a shot, pumping the lever. 'Waco, Chino! We're comin' out. Move in! Move in and finish every one of them!'

*   *   *

Slattery shot at the two men who ran from the barn doors to its right corner. He missed, he knew, by the way they hugged the snow. He lay still and quiet, aware of the throb of pain in his shoulder for the first time now . . .

He was sure Murfee had been hit. Steve hadn't fired in the past three minutes. He might be dead or dying, and Slattery couldn't reach him. Four gunmen would come at him, two from either side of the barn. He pressed himself into the snow, offering them less of a target. He didn't feel the cold, paid no attention to the pain, picturing in his mind the slaughter that would take place inside the house if the killers were able to get past

184

him . . .

Slattery lay absolutely still. He could hear nothing except the wind and swirl of snow. No movement at either side of the barn, not a sound or motion from Murfee. Slattery choked back a cough. He began to shiver from the last roll through the high drift. He pressed his left hand against his shoulder and attempted to control his body, but he still shook.

He raised his head an inch, squinting, trying to see and concentrate on Goodlove and his three men, yet other thoughts swept through his mind—hazy pictures of his life, the plans he'd made, leading the trail drive up into this new land, a small cattle spread with Judy, good neighbors, people they cared about and who would be their friends and would care about them and their children. His fingers grew numb. He knew he wouldn't be able to work the lever and pull the trigger if he lay like this much longer. Judy. Judy . . . she'd had so much belief in him and what they would do with their lives. She'd had so much hope . . .

The blurred forms of men, two of them, materialized from the left side of the barn, darker against the white of the snow. He sighted on the closer one. Before he could make his finger squeeze, more boots plodded through the deep drifts, and on the right the shadowy bodies of the third and fourth gunmen came into view, bent forward, their weapons out and ready.

Ketchuck's yells shocked Slattery. The man suddenly stood from the snowdrift that had hidden him, his arms raised high, his voice screaming against the wind.

'He's over there, Ralph! Get Slattery, Ralph. He's—'

A quick-triggered shot by the nearest figure cut off the words. The impact of the bullet knocked Ketchuck tumbling backwards as a rifle banged from the spot where Murfee had fallen. Slattery fired, rolled to his right, his half-frozen hands straining to pump the lever.

He was weak and cold and kept rolling, fighting to clash the cartridge into the chamber, hearing the fusillade of shots—three, four, a fifth and sixth—and bullets burning the air, tearing into the snow where he'd just been.

He had the weapon ready, jerked back on the trigger, sent the lead-jacketed slug at the single hazy target he could see.

Echoes of the gunfire died while the man went down. There was silence, except for the wind that whipped icy snow into his face while the cold gripped his fingers.

Then he heard a moan, a low, agonized groan from somewhere between him and the barn.

Silence again.

A voice said weakly, 'Chino's dead, Mr. Goodlove.' It was Waco Jones. 'I'm hit, Mr. Goodlove.'

'Back inside,' Goodlove answered, hidden

by the drifts near the barn. 'They killed Dancer.'

'I'm hit bad.' Another moan, weaker. 'Help me.'

Steve Murfee said from Slattery's left, 'I'll take Jones, Tom. He tries to move, he's dead.'

Slattery exhaled, breathed easier, knowing Murfee was all right.

The wind slackened a moment. In the quiet the soft crunch of a body crawling in the snow became a loud noise.

'Goodlove,' Jones pleaded. 'Help!'

The moving sounds stopped. Goodlove said, 'Cover me. I'm going back inside.'

'Sonofabitch!' Jones cried. 'Goodlove, I hope they get you, you bastard!' And very weak, 'Help. Help me.'

Then, again, only the wind and touch of snow broke the quiet.

* * *

Goodlove lay absolutely still. He'd heard Jones' swearing, his curse, but swearing and curses did not matter.

Nor did Slattery's shouts, 'Stand up, Goodlove! Drop your gun!'

He was hidden by the storm, as Slattery and Murfee had been hidden. Keeping his body low, he could reach the barn, get inside, and escape on one of the horses. Two of his men were dead, Jones so badly wounded he was of no help. The only decision was to run. He'd been so close to finishing off Slattery when Ketchuck's wild yells made him fire too soon. Everything had changed. His men were down, and Slattery and Murfee believed they'd won.

But they hadn't won. The storm would hold everyone inside the ranchhouse. Once he reached his ranch, he had ten more men who'd ride back and finish the job with him.

He began to crawl, his body sprawled flat, the Winchester carbine held above the snow to keep the action from becoming frozen and sluggish.

Goodlove glanced across his shoulder when he heard Murfee call, 'I've got Jones, Tom!' and he saw only one man followed him. Slattery! Terror gripped him. He was alone, all alone, and he had to get away! Turning, pushing up onto one knee, he fired, pumped, and squeezed again, then he made a dash for the high barn doors.

*   *   *

Slattery threw himself flat, feeling a bullet tug and rip through his coat, hearing the other slug burn past his head. Goodlove had lost control of himself, his shots fired wildly, but he could still kill and had to be approached carefully. Slattery pushed his body upward. He shook snow from his Winchester and brushed the icy wetness from his eyes. Goodlove had opened the barn door and now closed it behind him. Slattery continued to follow. He plodded through a high drift, then stopped at Murfee's call.

'Go 'round the back, Tom! I'll take the front!'

Snow covered almost all of Dancer's body. A second mound of drifted snow showed where Chino Neill lay. Waco Jones knelt in the whiteness, one arm raised in surrender, the other gripped tight to his side. Slattery motioned with his carbine. 'Take Jones in, Steve.'

'Me? Who's goin' to help me?' Ketchuck sat in the snow, looking up at Slattery and Murfee. 'He hit my leg! I was shot in the leg!'

'Take them both,' Slattery told Murfee. He could see the lawman limped, using his Spencer rifle held stock-down as a crutch to stay on his feet. 'You all right, Steve?'

Before Murfee could answer, Ketchuck cried, 'I need help! I can't walk!'

'You better walk,' Slattery snapped. And to Murfee, 'He expected them to let him go. Make him tell you why.'

Then Slattery walked on, bent forward, the carbine heavy and awkward in his stiffened fingers ...

The barn door had been shut tight, but streaks of lamplight showed at the top and above and below the hinges. Such a big barn, so much larger than the house. Slattery knew

Goodlove's greed, his drive for land and power, though he hadn't really ever spoken to the man. Goodlove hadn't done much talking in town or to the settlers he'd helped. The gunfighters he'd hired were easier to understand, taking their pay to live the way they'd chosen. He'd known so many gunfighters, had faced so many, and they'd usually talked a lot. You could usually figure what they'd do.

But not someone driven by the greed of a Goodlove. Slattery stopped at the doors, crouched down, and listened. He could barely move his fingers. The cold numbed his neck and shoulder. He took his right hand off the carbine, flexed the fingers. He could feel his wound again, a deep thrust of pain which stabbed up into his head and down along his arms . . .

Sounds inside the barn made him forget that—the whinny of a horse, the kicks of a horse's hoofs.

Slattery gripped the rope door handle and pulled hard. He moved inside, stayed low, the carbine in both hands while he kept moving to the left away from the opening. Goodlove had Ketchuck's horse saddled. He led it down the aisle between the stalls toward the barn's rear, his back turned, one hand reaching out to push open the door.

'Stop!' Slattery called. 'Drop your gun, Goodlove!'

190

The rancher whirled on his bootheels, his carbine leveled, flashing, exploding. Bullets sprayed the aisle. They smashed into the stallbeams, the rafters and the door behind Slattery. One slug ricocheted crazily off an iron hinge as Slattery used every last bit of his strength to make his frozen finger squeeze the trigger of his Winchester carbine.

CHAPTER TWENTY

Inside the house, everyone waited and watched the closed kitchen door.

Mal Weaver sat at the table, his Colt revolver in his hand. The bandage his wife had wrapped around the bullet burn above his left ear pressed on the wound, making his head ache. He tried to calm the ache by not moving, but the soreness didn't lessen.

'It's so quiet out there,' he said. 'Steve, we ought to go see.'

'You can't go out,' his wife told him quickly. She'd believed he was dead when he'd fallen, his hair drenched with blood, and she was thankful the bullet had only grazed and stunned him. She dropped the soggy blood-soaked towel she had used to clean the wound into the water bucket. 'If you move, you'll start bleeding again.'

'But it's too quiet. Goodlove could've killed

191

Tom.'

Murfee, leaning with his back pressed against the wall directly opposite the door, said, 'We don't leave. He did get Tom, he'll be tryin' to come in.'

He'd chosen the spot opposite the door so he'd be the first to see who'd won in the barn. His thigh was sore where a bullet had torn the flesh, but as long as he kept his weight on his spine, flush against the wall, he could stand and use his Spencer rifle.

Lottie Wells, sitting with Judy in the front room, held Linda Weaver close to her. Waco Jones lay in the far corner of the kitchen, both of his hands gripping his side. Murfee hadn't let the women close to him, not wanting them in the line of fire until he was certain Slattery would be the one to come in . . . He looked down at Ketchuck crouched against the wall, his face pasty white, his legs still trembling from being shot by Goodlove.

'And Goodlove took ownership of every one of those ranches that way?' Murfee asked the land agent. 'He meant to push us all out one by one and take our land?'

Ketchuck's thin shoulders shuddered and he nodded. 'But I didn't have anythin' to do with the killings. I didn't.' He stared at Waco Jones as though he was filled with disgust simply looking at him. 'He shot me in the knee! They meant to kill me! They must have planned that all along. To kill me!'

192

'You'll appear in court?' Murfee said.

'I will! I'll tell what I know, even about Goodlove building big barns so he'd have plenty room to store his hay!' His stare rose, moved from face to face, from Murfee to Judy Fiske and Lottie and the Weavers and their daughter. The child was terrified, holding tight to Lottie, but Ketchuck was aware of only his own shock and hurt. 'I didn't do anything to be shot. I was in on the land deals but not the killings.'

He was going to add more when Murfee motioned for him to be quiet. The crunch of boots in the snow sounded outside. Everyone stiffened, watching the door. Murfee's rifle was centered on the door. Weaver held his Colt in both hands, his arms resting on the table top to level the muzzle at the same spot as Murfee.

The crunch of boots moved up onto the back stoop. A hand gripped the doorknob and the knob began to turn.

'Tom?' Murfee questioned.

'Yes, Steve.' Slattery opened the door and stepped into the room. He scanned the faces, first Judy, then Lottie and the small girl, past the Weavers to Murfee and Ketchuck. He glanced from Ketchuck to Waco Jones, then again at the child. Linda's small round cheeks were flushed red and there was swelling around her eyes from crying. 'There's no one left out there,' he told the little girl. 'No one

193

can hurt you.'

Judy Fiske said, 'All of them? Ralph Goodlove?'

Nodding, Slattery laid the Winchester flat on the table. For a moment he watched Judy. Then he studied Weaver's bandaged head and Murfee's bloody pants leg.

Murfee leaned on the Spencer rifle. 'See to Jones,' he told Lottie. He motioned down at Ketchuck. 'He was in on it, Tom. He'll testify before a judge.'

'I wasn't responsible for what happened here.' The agent gripped his knee, pain in his eyes. 'They tried to kill me too!' He jerked his head up and down briskly and added, 'I didn't know about the Colburns. Or about McDonald and Huffaker!'

An instant dead hush filled the room. Linda Weaver backed away from him toward her mother and father. Slattery asked, 'What about Huffaker and McDonald?'

Ketchuck cowered more, edging away from Murfee, as though he feared he might be kicked. The same open fear lined his face. 'I didn't know,' he began. 'I was in the valley when Goodlove sent Dancer and Jones out. Churchill was there too. He didn't break his leg. One of them shot him, and Goodlove made it look like he got hurt on his ranch.'

Every face turned to Jones. Lottie Wells had his coat off and shirt unbuttoned. She stopped helping him at Ketchuck's words. Slattery

194

walked to the corner where the gunman lay.

Jones shook his head before Slattery could ask a question. 'Dancer shot them,' he said. 'I was with Jim Dancer. We waited out in the brush and saw them talkin' to Cal Teller. When the drummer pushed on, we rode in on them. We told them to ride out, but they wouldn't. Dancer drew and did the shooting. Marsh Churchill was there. It happened so quick, neither Marsh or me had time to draw. The one named Huffaker got a shot off and hit Marsh.' His face had taken on the same fear as Linda Weaver had shown. 'We dumped both of them and their horses off the cliff and then we brought Marsh in with the story he'd broken his leg.'

A heavy silence hung over the listeners, the single audible sound was the low sigh of their breathing. Linda Weaver pressed against her mother. Her father took the child's hand.

Jones stared up into Murfee's face, then at Slattery. 'Look, I'm tellin' you—' His mouth closed tight as Slattery snapped, 'You'll tell! In court!' He stood over the wounded man. Jones edged away from him. He realized he'd doubled both his fists and leaned forward as though he'd lash out at the gunman's face. He straightened, looking at Ketchuck. 'You'll appear in court. You won't change your story.'

'No. No, I won't.'

Slattery looked from the land agent to the Weavers and then at Steve Murfee who again leaned back flush against the wall staring down at Waco Jones.

Jones made a low, whimpering sound. He took his hands from his side, showing his own blood on his fingers. 'I was shot! Look, I'm hit bad!'

'Shut up!' Murfee snapped. The lawman straightened now, his uninjured leg set solidly against the floor to hold his weight. But he did not make a motion toward either Ketchuck or Jones. 'Just you shut up! Both of you!'

Judy Fiske watched Slattery. 'Tom, you'll want to go to the Huffakers,' she said. 'When the storm is over. I'll go with you.'

Slattery took two short steps to Judy's chair. She sat with both of her hands in her lap. She was tired and drawn and as shocked and hurt as he and the others at hearing about Fred McDonald and Ian Huffaker. But he saw more than that in her eyes, something that had been there the first time that he'd met her and during all the long, hard days and nights of the trail drive into this Montana high country. He held out his hands to her.

'You got up once to help,' he said. 'Help yourself now.'

She made no motion to take his fingers. 'Tom, I told you about Ralph. I—'

'I didn't hear,' Slattery said.

He moved a few inches closer and Judy reached out and gripped his outstretched hands. Slowly, he drew her up onto her feet,

196

facing him. She kept looking directly into his eyes and neither of them spoke another word, even after he let go of her hands and she was standing alone.